DUSK OR DAWN
BY
EJ Raymond

(C) Copyrighted 2021

To three lovely women: 'T', Margaret (my mum… who not read full thing, wish me luck!) and Rachel Amey - a massive thank you for ensure my story's English look good! And also to wonderful Philippa Tomlin for your hard work to made a cover of this book, Thank you!

PROLOGUE

It was very dark in the busy street outside one of the gay nightclubs in the centre of Manchester's popular Gay Village. A beautiful woman in her late thirties walked out of her regular nightclub. She wore a gentleman-style suit that she was really proud of. Her face showed a bit of disappointment because it wasn't her lucky night; she hadn't pulled anyone in the nightclub. She sighed and walked very calmly into an alleyway. As she brought her lighter up to her cigarette, she heard someone running close by behind her. She turned around but there was no one there. At first, she was terrified but then sighed and felt annoyed. She wasn't aware that someone was running along the top of the building above her.

"Bloody rats." she said to herself as she tried to light her cigarette.

She heard footsteps, running and approaching her. She turned quickly to try and catch the person, but no one was around.

"Rats, fuck off!" she snapped furiously. She sighed again and turned around. She saw a person standing in front of her which gave her a real fright. "Shit! Fucking hell! You scared me to death!"

"Is that so?" said a gentleman's voice with a very posh English accent.

"Sorry?" The woman was puzzled

"Rats. That's what you called us, rats?"

"Oh, no, I heard a noise but I just assumed it was coming from rats," the woman mumbled.

"Oh, I apologise for frightening you," the gentleman said as his face appeared in the streetlight. It terrified the woman. All of his skin looked very pale. He wore a long-length black leather jacket, which matched his black hair and narrow beard. He looked up and down the woman's suit. "…Madam?"

The woman looked down and realised that the gentleman was puzzled about her gender.

"It's she." she confirmed.

"Ah, very well." he smirked, "I'm Yves."

"Um… Sinead." Sinead's voice was shaking because she felt so uncomfortable. She realised that she was not alone; some more men and women were standing behind Yves. They were all wearing clothes that were similar to Yves'. Sinead turned her head and saw more people behind her. She noticed that all of them were as pale-looking as Yves was.

"Ah, Sinead," Yves smirked again.

"Y-y-you can have my money." Sinead removed her small purse out of her suit pocket.

"How nice of you," Yves let out a small laugh, "but, no thanks."

"What do you want?" Sinead tried to stay calm but inside she felt really panicked.

"Say please, then I'll tell you."

Sinead looked at the people who had surrounded her; they terrified her. Clearing her throat, she said, "Sir… please tell me what you want from me."

"How polite. Well, in fact, what we really want is… **you**."

Sinead's eyes widened with horror.

"Your blood."

Sinead realised that she was surrounded by vampires so she stepped backwards in terror.

"Then you'll become like the rest of us. Is that too much to ask?" Yves continued.

Sinead searched for somewhere to escape but it was impossible.

Yves sighed with impatience, "My friend… we cannot wait any longer for your response." He turned to the others, "Take her."

The vampires popped out their fangs, ran, and flew towards Sinead.

"NO!!" Sinead screamed.

The Gay Village street was busy, full of LGBTQI+ people who passed by the alleyway. They hardly heard Sinead's screams through loud music from every pub and nightclub as the vampires pushed her down on to the ground.

Yves stood there, watching. Sinead's screaming continued, her face looked as horrified as a bright - white moon.

CHAPTER ONE
DUSK - THREE WEEKS LATER…

There were many people, especially children, walking around in a park where a carnival had been set up for almost a week. There were very bright, colourful light bulbs above the stalls, bright enough to welcome the excited people as they walked through the dark night.

Two ladies in their late thirties, Rose Lynch and Cara Miles, stood behind one of the carnival games tents. Cara threw a ball and knocked down all ten of the empty tins. Rose screamed with joy, excited that Cara had won a prize.

A man gave her a cuddly rabbit as her prize. "Congratulations!"

"Thank you!" said Cara in her deaf voice. Cara had been profoundly deaf since birth, as explained to her by her mother. She hugged her new cuddly rabbit and noticed someone small staring at her. She turned and saw a little boy looking up with sad, puppy-eyes. She smiled sympathetically and knelt on the ground at eye-level with the little boy. She raised one of her eyebrows, shaking the cuddly rabbit before giving it to him.

The little boy gasped, "For me?!"

"Yes, you," said Cara.

"Thank you!" The boy turned to his mother, "Mummy, look! That lady gave me this!"

"Ah, that's so lovely!" his mother cooed. She looked at Cara, silently mouthing - *Are you sure?*

Cara lip read her and nodded.

"Thank you." She smiled, heartened, and turned to her son, "Go on, say 'thank you' to her."

The little boy came closer to Cara and hugged her. Cara laughed, feeling as well heartened.

Rose stood there and saw the whole thing.

"Lovely boy," Cara told the mother.

"He must get it from his father!" The mother laughed, so did Cara, "Say bye to her."

"Bye-bye!" responded the little boy, hugging his cuddly rabbit tightly.

Cara laughed, waving to them until they went out of sight.

"How did you know every word that she said?" Rose signed.

"Her lips were really clear to lip-read," Cara answered.

"Oh, fair enough." Rose held Cara's hand as they walked around to search for something that they would like to do. "That was nice of you, giving away your prize to that cute little boy." Rose was impressed. "Anyway, how are you getting on with your boss?"

Cara made a 'bleurgh' sound.

"No good?" asked Rose.

"Worse. He's freaking me out big time!" Cara shook her head and laughed.

"Why not just tell him that you're gay, it's that simple," Rose suggested.

"He will find out somehow."

"Ok. Anyway, let's forget about our jobs, let's go and have fun!"

"You read my mind!" agreed Cara, kissing Rose's lips. They walked arm-in-arm as they headed for more fun.

* * * * *

Later that night, Rose and Cara were in Rose's bedroom, lying on her king-size bed. Rose was kissing Cara all over. They were both almost naked except Rose wore women's underwear and Cara wore a pair of men's boxer shorts and a t-shirt.

Rose's fingers started to climb down and into Cara's boxers. Cara pushed Rose's hand away from her boxers as they continued to kiss. Rose moved her lips down Cara's neck, they moaned. Rose decided to go under Cara's t-shirt and kissed on Cara's upper body which made Cara moan. Rose pulled herself further down.

"Stop," Cara warned.

Rose ignored her or pretended that she hadn't heard. She continued to kiss Cara over the top of her boxer shorts, just above Cara's private parts. "Stop…" Cara repeated. Her voice sounded like she was about to cry. Rose put her fingers inside the boxers. "No… NO!" Cara pushed Rose away, then started to use her sign language, "STOP! I've told you - DON'T!"

Cara got off the bed and grabbed her jeans.

"Oh come on," said Rose defensively, "Cara, What's the matter?"

Cara pushed her legs into her jeans and pulled them upwards. She sighed. "You've gone too far."

Rose got off the bed to get close to Cara. "That's me, Rose." She kissed Cara to apologise to her. They started kissing again. Rose put her hand near Cara's private parts again.

Cara pushed her away in fury, "I have to go." She only spoke - she didn't bother to use sign language as she walked out of Rose's room.

"What?" Rose exclaimed, with her arms raised in the air in confusion.

Cara slammed the front door and walked out of Rose's house. She was so frustrated with herself for not liking sex with women as Rose did. She walked along, down the street, all the while hitting herself and grunting. Out of the blue, heavy rain started to pour from the sky.

Cara gasped in surprise, breathless when she finally stopped hurting herself. She watched the thunderstorm and wished a lighting bolt would strike her down dead. She stood on the wet road for a good few minutes, to let out all of her crying.

Twenty minutes had passed, it was still raining, but even more heavily. Cara's arms were crossed against her chest as she walked along in sorrow. She was only wearing her t-shirt and jeans as she had left her jacket back at Rose's. She was shivering and coughing. She wasn't aware that someone had appeared behind her; they stood still and watched. Cara was completely soaked and her teeth were chattering as she arrived at the footpath in front of her house. She pulled her keys out of the pocket of her soaked jeans before she arrived at her front door. Her hands were shaking and her teeth chattering had become worse. The keys slipped out of her hand and fell on the doorstep.

Cara gave out a heavy sigh; she was so exhausted and weak. She bent down to pick up the keys and searched for the right key. As she straightened up she felt puzzled, she was pretty sure that she could feel someone there, so she turned around.

"Argh - fuck!" Cara jumped with her hand held to her chest, her heart thumping as though she was having a massive heart attack.

Sinead stood there, just watching her. Her face was far too pale, she wore black leather clothes like Yves and his group of vampires.

Cara laughed at being so frightened for those few seconds and looked up at Sinead.

Their eyes meet.

Cara's face suddenly dropped.

Sinead smirked.

"Oh, shit!" Cara whispered to herself. She put the key into the keyhole as quickly as she could, opened the door to get in and slam it shut. But her plan didn't go well. Sinead pushed the door wide open with such force that the edge of the door banged against Cara's head.

Cara fell to the floor and groaned. Her forehead was bleeding. She looked up at Sinead walking towards her. Cara crawled backwards in fear.

"How...?" Cara whimpered.

"How?" Sinead asked to make sure that she picked up Cara's deaf voice.

Cara got up from the floor and ran into her kitchen.

Sinead shrugged, thinking that this woman must have changed her mind about asking the question.

Cara ran behind the kitchen table, trying to get away from Sinead.

Suddenly Sinead stood right in front of Cara and Cara screamed.

Sinead put her thumb on Cara's forehead and wiped away Cara's blood. She then licked the blood.

"What the fuck?!" Cara was shocked because she had never seen Sinead like that before.

Sinead's fangs started to show. Cara froze and gasped.

"Why don't you run?" Sinead said and smirked.

Cara managed to push Sinead away and went straight to one of the kitchen drawers.

Sinead turned where she had been standing and then moved so fast that within a blink of an eye she was close behind Cara's back. She pinned Cara's face down onto the floor. As Sinead's fangs came closer to Cara's neck, she heard a loud, laboured breath coming from Cara. The sound of her gasp wasn't good. Sinead turned Cara's body over and saw a big kitchen knife stuck in her belly.

Cara was bleeding badly, she gasped because she couldn't catch her breath. The knife had gone up into one of her lungs. Cara's face had turned so pale that it was a perfect match to Sinead's skin.

"...Why?" Cara whimpered, frightened that she was going to die.

Sinead shook her head because she had no idea what Cara was trying to say.

"Sinead... please... leave me alone," Cara cried breathlessly.

Sinead suddenly recognised the imperfect pronunciation of her name.

Her fangs disappeared back into her teeth.

Cara saw this happen. She was so shocked that she forgot for a minute that she was lying there dying.

"Leigh? Is that you?" Sinead was puzzled.

Cara didn't understand what Sinead had said. She tried to speak carefully so that Sinead could understand, "How - did - you - find - me?"

But Sinead didn't understand Cara either.

"What? What are you trying to say?"

"How..." Cara didn't manage to finish her sentence. She didn't have enough oxygen left in her body to stay conscious and so she blacked out.

CHAPTER TWO

There was an area of empty ground that had been closed down for many, many years. There were lumps of what looked like mounds of coals covered in grassy weeds everywhere. Beneath it was an old, empty mine that had been abandoned long ago. This was where Sinead had been hiding, along with thousands of other vampires, throughout the daylight hours.

In Sinead's own personal 'space/room', she sat on what looked like a chair made of rocks.

She was staring at nothing; her mind kept bothering her.

Cara collapsed on Sinead's arm; Sinead grunted with frustration. She forced her hand onto Cara's wound and another hand onto the knife and then slowly pulled the knife backwards.

Cara gasped before waking up. She silently screamed out while she grabbed Sinead's wrist.

"Hold on!" Sinead said, then ripped Cara's t-shirt and put it into her mouth to stop her from screaming. Sinead then grabbed a kitchen towel and pressed it around Cara's wound, ready to pull the full length of the knife out of her belly. Cara's screams were muffled by the cloth in her mouth. Sinead quickly moved her hand over Cara's mouth to stop the sound. Cara was crying in pain and fear. With her other hand, Sinead moved the kitchen towel away from

Cara's belly. She then put more pressure on the bleeding wound.

Cara stared at Sinead's hand resting on her belly. A glow came from Sinead's hand and onto her wound.

Cara's eyesight became blurred before she rolled backwards and blacked out again.

Sinead carried Cara into the bedroom and carefully put her onto the bed. She pulled the duvet over Cara and noticed an old scar on her right shoulder. The scar reminded Sinead of many years before when she was young and was hanging out with her gang of boys. They were all poking broken metal poles towards Leigh. One of the boys went too far and forced the pole through the skin of Leigh's shoulder. Leigh looked down and cried. Her shoulder was bleeding; she collapsed on the grass and blacked out. The young gang soon stopped laughing when they realised what they had done. Everyone except Sinead ran away. She watched Leigh's face.

Sinead remembered what happened with guilt written all over her face. She picked up Cara's wallet and took the card out.

"Cara Miles." Sinead read Cara's I.D. out loud.

Sinead covered her face, feeling guilty, "I'm so sorry, Leigh," she whispered to herself.

"What's the matter, my friend?" Yves' voice interrupted Sinead's thoughts.

"Nothing." Sinead sighed.

Yves walked into Sinead's room with a smile showing on his pale face, "Go on, tell me."

Sinead looked at Yves with an exhausted smile. She knew it was pointless for her to complain that she didn't belong there, she didn't want to be a vampire. She couldn't blame him for ordering his vampire gang to attack her, because if she argued back, Yves would use his power against her.

"Give me time, Yves," Sinead said and forced out a smile.

"Hmm. Try to be chilled, my friend," Yves replied. He could sense that Sinead was hiding something. "However… if you want to give up, there are two simple choices: Dusk or dawn. If you choose dusk, you stay a vampire for the rest of your life. Or, if you choose dawn, you will never see the world ever again. So… it's your decision to make." He smiled then left.

Sinead was boiling up inside, not at all pleased about her difficult choice. She didn't want to stay a vampire, but she wanted to find out more about Leigh, whom she believed to have been dead for many years. Suddenly she heard squeaking and saw rats crawling about on the ground. She grabbed one of them for her 'breakfast'.

CHAPTER THREE

Cara murmured in her bed. Her body was soaked with sweat. She had a recurring, echoing dream.

Sinead appeared with her pale face and fangs showing... Four boys and a girl looked down and laughed... The knife stabbed into her belly... A boy is dressing up as a vampire, he looked so determined and grabbed... Both teenagers Leigh and Sinead got close for a kiss... Suddenly 'adult' Sinead's face with her fangs showing came out of nowhere into Cara's view.

Cara screamed and woke herself up.

"Hey, hey, hey - that's ok! It's just a nightmare," said Rose to comfort her.

Cara was breathless, still sweating, her body shivered.

"Why are you here?" she signed.

"Your boss -"

"Shit!" Cara panicked, she realised that she was late for work. She pushed the duvet away and was about to get up but Rose pushed her back on the bed again. Cara groaned. "Fuck... Ow." She winced because her body ached so much.

"You can't go to work like that!" exclaimed Rose.

Cara coughed violently.

"You're not feeling so well, it's best you stay in bed," continued Rose. Cara winced in pain again. "I'll call a doctor to come up here and check on you."

"No... no doctor." Cara shook her head and whimpered.

"Seriously?" Rose raised an eyebrow. Cara nodded; her eyes looked like she was half asleep.

"All right, babe, it's your choice. Stay in bed 'til you're feeling much better, yeah?" Rose warned. Cara just nodded; she wished Rose would just shut the fuck up and leave. "Ok... I'll check on you tomorrow, alright?"

"Mmm." Cara rolled herself into her duvet and the pillows.

"Love you."

Cara shut her eyes. Rose sighed; she'd never heard Cara say the 'L' word once in their two-year relationship. She got up and kissed Cara's forehead before leaving the room.

* * * * *

Some hours had passed - Cara continued to toss and turn in her sleep, still sweating and mumbling.

Sinead stood outside Cara's front door; she looked up to meet Cara's eyes.

Cara continued moaning and grunting.

Sinead opened her mouth, revealing fangs as she prepared bite Cara's neck.

Seeing Sinead's fangs frightened Cara big time, her fear forced her to wake up gasping and breathless.

At first, she struggled to catch her breath but then she felt calmer. She grunted, her body still full of pain as if she had the flu. She thought she noticed a figure out of the corner of her eye. She turned and saw Sinead sat on a chair at the back of the room, smiling.

"What's the matter?"

Cara got off the bed. She fell on the floor and crawled backwards, hitting her head against the wall. Her heart was pounding fast. She looked around the room; there was no sign of Sinead. Sighing, she slowly climbed back up onto the bed and hit her head on the pillow. "Stupid dream," she murmured, still shivering with the cold. She turned over to the other side of the bed and opened her tired eyes.

Sinead lay on the bed next to Cara and smiled. "What was your dream about?" She mimed as she wasn't good with sign language. Suddenly her hand clasped Cara's mouth: she saw that Cara was so terrified that she was about to scream. "Shush. Please… don't be frightened, I'm not going to hurt you." Sinead spoke as clearly as possible hoping that Cara would understand her. Cara stiffened in terror. "You're not going to scream?" Sinead asked her again using mime. Cara eagerly shook her head no. "Promise?" Sinead was still uncertain but Cara nodded quickly. Sinead slowly took her hand away from Cara's mouth.

Cara's whole body was shaking.

"Don't be afraid," Sinead said calmly.

"I can't help it." Cara finally spoke, pulling the duvet over herself, "Anyway, how did you find out where I lived?"

"I know that sign… no, I just… a random walk… in that… road. I… saw you walking." Sinead tried to explain using speech and mime.

Cara groaned and covered the duvet over her whole body. She was shocked to see that Sinead was also under the duvet. Cara got off the bed and walked backwards.

Sinead pushed the duvet away from her and followed Cara.

"What's that?!" Cara shouted, pointing at the duvet, "How?!"

Sinead sighed, "It's magic."

"Magic?" said Cara, breathlessly.

"Hmm."

"Who *are* you?"

"It's me, Sinead."

"I know!" Cara suddenly coughed violently, "But, what the fuck are you?!"

"Fine. I'm a vampire." Sinead put both of her index fingers on her lips to mime 'Vampire'.

Cara's eyes widened.

"Don't… you promised me -" Sinead suddenly zoomed towards Cara and forced her hand over Cara's mouth, just as she was about to open it to scream out. "I know, I take it that you remembered last night."

Cara sobbed, she was terrified.

"Hey, shh… I'm not going to hurt you," Sinead shushed.

Cara signed something but Sinead didn't catch what it was so she released Cara's mouth, "Say it again?"

"What do you want from me?" asked Cara, sobbing.

"Erm… I just want to be your friend, that's all."

"No way."

"No way? Why?"

"You're a vampire!"

"Look, I'm not going to bite you."

"You don't understand!"

"Try me!"

"I'm s-a-n-g…." Cara seemed to really struggle with using fingerspelling, she sighed furiously. She then tried to write it down on a piece of paper but it was impossible to spell it either.

"What are you trying to say?" asked Sinead, puzzled.

That word really frustrated her. Cara gave up and instead wrote down a simple explanation on the piece of paper.

"'Afraid of vampires'? Obviously, everyone is afraid of us," scoffed Sinead. Cara realised that she had put the wrong word down, so she wrote again. "…phobia of them? You? Even on Halloween night?" asked Sinead, puzzled after reading Cara's handwriting.

Cara looked away and nodded.

Sinead turned Cara back round to face her, "Why?"

Cara had a flashback of a teenage boy who wore vampire clothes and had black paint on his hair. His painted face was as pale as a ghost. He smiled, smirking, with his fangs showing. Thinking of it made Cara panic; she shook her head.

Sinead caught Cara before she collapsed to avoid hitting her head on the floor. "You're burning."

"I'm not so well," winced Cara.

"It must've been the rain last night," said Sinead to herself.

"Sinead."

"What?"

"Why-are-you-here?" Cara repeated the same question, moaning.

"I don't know. After - seeing - you - last night. I thought - you… erm… yummy." Sinead explained using mime. Cara was puzzled. Sinead sighed then showed her fangs. Cara suddenly froze. "Oh, shit!" Sinead put her hand on her mouth, "I'm so sorry!" She said after her fangs disappeared again. Then she wrote down on the paper, murmuring. "When you said my name, I recognised your voice." She showed the paper to Cara but Cara's vision was now so blurred that she couldn't read the words. This confused her.

"Leigh?"

Cara shut her eyelids.

"Leigh!" Sinead lifted Cara and put her on the bed. She then lifted the bottom of Cara's t-shirt and saw a large infection over the scar on Cara's belly.

Cara woke again. She looked down to see what Sinead was looking at and noticed the scar. She was breathless with confusion.

"This is a dream. I'm not well… I… this is just a dream!" Cara murmured. Squeezing her eyelids shut, she started to cry.

Sinead pressed her hand onto Cara's scar and closed her eyes. Her hand glowed as it connected to the scar.

Cara opened her eyes suddenly, she grabbed Sinead's wrist and gasped. She saw the past in fast-motion images that terrified her - *Sinead attacked her, she was stabbed. The images then fast forwarded to when Sinead showed her fangs.*

Sinead stopped what she was doing. The scar on Cara's skin had become smaller.

Cara gasped loudly and breathlessly, looked at Sinead. Sinead saw tears run down Cara's cheeks.

"Please… me - no - vampire…" Cara whimpered.

Sinead grabbed the pen and paper and wrote down: 'Don't worry, I'm only trying to heal you. I will look after you, to make sure you will not become one.' She showed it to Cara.

Cara struggled to read it at first, Sinead decided to use her vampire powers to help Cara see better, so she placed her palm on Cara's forehead. Cara could then clearly see the paper. She read it and looked up at Sinead, uncertainty showing on her face.

"I promised," said Sinead, crossing her heart.

Cara nodded and grunted.

Sinead pressed her hand upon Cara's belly where the scar was.

Cara's tears flowed as the flashback returned when Sinead's hand glowed with the connection to Cara's scar. Cara saw four boys and a girl staring down at her and laughing. It went over and over in her mind.

Sinead's hand stopped glowing - Cara's scar had completely disappeared from her belly.

Cara looked at Sinead's guilty face then burst into tears.

Sinead pulled Cara towards her to hug her and to let out her crying. Holding her close, Sinead could hear a rhythmic pulsing sound near one of her ears. She turned and looked at Cara's neck. Her eyes darted to watch Cara's neck veins pumping - *boom boom*. Sinead quickly turned her head away and tightly shut her eyelids to avoid temptation.

Outside Cara's bedroom window Yves was standing in the air, watching them. It didn't please him, at all.

CHAPTER FOUR

The next morning, the sun beamed through the curtains which she hadn't shut properly. Cara slept peacefully all night, her sweating and nightmares disappeared as if they'd never existed. She yawned and looked around her room; it was nice and clear which was just how she liked it. She looked at the clock on the bedside table next to her bed: 07:00. She exhaled, thinking about the day ahead.

*****

Cara walked in the kitchen wearing her Royal Mail uniform. She put her daily tablet into her mouth and drank some water to force it down her throat. She noticed a piece of paper on the table, she was puzzled so approached and read it:

Sorry I have to go before dawn. Hope to see you again tonight. Sinead x

Cara started to panic. She grabbed a small mirror from one of her drawers to check her neck over. All of her skin was smooth - no pale tone, scars, marks, or anything. She turned towards the kitchen table and frowned. The paper was blank; there wasn't a single drop of ink written on it. It made her so confused that she shook her head, "Don't be stupid!" she signed to herself, grabbing her mailbag and leaving.

The message had appeared, written with lipstick, and then disappeared, leaving the paper blank.

* * * * *

Cara entered the Royal Mail mailroom to pick up loads of envelopes from the shelves and put them in her bag before getting more envelopes.

Her boss who was in his late thirties appeared, smiling politely. He had a small bald patch above his forehead. He was an awkward, almost shy person. He had fancied Cara for a long time, ever since Cara had started working for Royal Mail. Cara, however, found him very annoying. He tried too hard to impress her with sign language which he believed he was really good at, but in Cara's eyes, he was just mocking her with sign language.

"You… OK? Sick?" said her boss with his hopeless signing skills.

"I'm fine, thank you," Cara signed quickly with a fake smile.

"Oh, good… good to hear - no, no… good to *see* you ok."

"I have to go." Cara pointed her index finger outwards, she turned around, rolled her eyes, and walked away just before her boss was about to say something.

"…Right," the boss whispered to himself, then winced, "Damn it."

"You owe me a fiver, boss." A postman turned up, smirking with his hand held open, waiting for money to be laid on it.

Sighing, the boss put the cash in the postman's hand.

"Cheers! Oh, before I forget... Umm... Thought you'd better know that... How can I put this..." The postman cleared his throat, "She's not into dicks."

The boss turned slowly and realised what the postman meant. "Like...?"

"Hmm. Pussies only. She's gay." The postman clarified before he burst out laughing and walked away.

The boss was so shocked; he couldn't have possibly embarrassed himself any more than he had.

* * * * *

Rose was driving her beloved sports car and singing her heart out along to the car radio. Her singing became quieter and her pitch lower as she looked out in surprise. She saw Cara walking along the pavement in her work uniform. Rose pulled over beside Cara to get her attention.

"What are you doing?" Rose scoffed. She couldn't believe she was seeing Cara out and about.

Cara looked at her in confusion, then looked at the envelopes that she held in her hand, trying to give Rose the hint that she was working.

"Hi," Cara frowned.

"'Hi'? Thought you were supposed to be staying at home, you know, in bed?"

"But I feel so great."

"Really?"

"*Really*." Cara responded very seriously.

"...Okay. Weird. Anyway, seeing as though you're up and about, I'm going to the carnival tonight - you coming? I heard today would be the last day."

"Why not," Cara answered without thinking.

"Awesome! What time do you want me to pick you up?"

"Nah, I'll meet you at the carnival at seven," Cara looked at the envelopes in her hand, "After work, I'll get a nap, shower then walk to the carnival."

"Alright, come here." Rose moved her index finger to encourage Cara to come closer to her lips to kiss. Rose pulled her closer for more and Cara let her. When their kissing ended, they smiled at each other, both feeling so heartened.

"Right, I have to go. Seven o'clock."

Cara nodded, they waved at each other before Rose drove away. Cara dropped her arm down and sighed.

Rose doesn't deserve it, she thought.

* * * * *

Rose stood waiting at the front of the entrance until Cara turned up at seven o'clock sharp; she kissed Rose's lips.

"Mmm." Rose felt so dizzy from feeling Cara's wet lips.

"Looks like it'll be really busy soon," said Cara, disturbing Rose's pleasurable moment.

"Erm, yes, yes it looks like it. Let's go!"

They went into the entrance arm-in-arm through the crowd of people. They spent a few good hours enjoying themselves around the carnival.

Towards the end of the evening, they stood in the queue outside the circus big tent.

"Babe," Rose got Cara's attention, "After that, I wonder if you would like to stay over at mine tonight?"

Cara looked down at the ground to avoid her question. Rose lifted Cara's chin to look at her. "Please? I miss you. I just want to wake up and see you by my side first thing in the morning."

Cara had a feeling that Rose was up to something that she was not ready for.

"You know, I'd love to but I'd better go straight home after this."

Rose dropped her shoulders in disappointment and sighed.

"I have to go to work tomorrow morning," continued Cara.

"Can we talk?" Rose looked so serious.

Uh-oh, Cara thought; she knew it was coming but forced herself to nod and be prepared to hear what her girlfriend was about to say.

"It's about two nights ago, you know?"

Cara turned her head away and sighed, thinking: *Fuck. Fuck. Fuck. Fuck.*

Rose put her hand on Cara's cheek and moved to look at her again, "You keep pushing me away. I thought we -"

"Whoa. Me, pushed you away? Tell me what you remember from when we first met?"

"That you don't like sex," Rose remembered.

"Yes, that's right. And now look at you, where's your respect?" Cara felt offended.

"Then why? Tell me!"

"Please stop. I don't want to talk about it, ok?"

"Look, we've been together for, what, two years? We need to be open with each other."

Cara shook her head.

"What's going on?" Rose grunted.

"Please just change the subject, yeah?"

"Are you seeing someone else?" Rose blunted out.

Cara gasped in horror, "How dare you say that?! No!"

"Then tell me!"

"I'm not seeing anyone, ok? But I don't want to fuck with you, or with anyone. OK?!" snapped Cara. She then noticed that people in the queue were staring at her. She realised that she had raised her voice loudly, "Sorry."

"I… I'm sorry… I…" Rose couldn't find the right words to say.

"Look, I told you on the first night we met. I. Don't. Like. Sex. That's it." Cara reminded her again.

"But I do," murmured Rose, "I miss sex."

"I know, I can tell."

"I've masturbated for two years but it's not the same…"

"You don't deserve to be with someone like me who hates having sex."

"I -" Rose opened her mouth to speak but then changed her mind.

"The line's open!" announced the staff, getting everyone's attention.

"I think we should split up," Rose suggested with a cold tone.

"Fine. I'd better go anyway. Have fun in there," Cara blunted as she turned and walked away. She handed her ticket out to a stranger.

"Oh, thank you!" The stranger said, very happily.

Rose watched Cara until she disappeared into the distance. She frowned before going into the tent.

Cara hugged herself, crying as she walked out of the carnival in the dark, alone.

Why must everything be about sex? She scoffed, feeling upset.

* * * * *

Cara arrived in her bedroom, exhausted.

"Hello, bed." She spoke to her bed in her deaf voice as if she and the bed were best friends. She removed her casual clothes and climbed onto the duvet, wearing just her t-shirt and boxers. She exhaled and collapsed on the mattress and hit her head hard on the pillow. She closed her eyes and fell deeply asleep. But the unpleasant dream started to come…

About an hour later, Sinead flew into Cara's bedroom window; she used her power to open it. She climbed into the window and walked on the carpet towards Cara's bed. Sinead stood beside the bed watching Cara in her sleep.

She remembered an event that happened over twenty-five years ago, at her primary school playground.

Young Sinead was hanging out with three friends, all boys, and her younger brother Brandon. They were all walking together until one of the friends, Peter, spotted young Leigh.

"There she is!" Bob, another gang member, got excited.

"Let's go and get her!" Jason, the third gang member, encouraged everyone to run.

Leigh was happily playing with one of her friends when her friend suddenly looked up in horror before turning away in a hurry. Leigh was confused, looking round for what she'd missed. She saw five bullies running towards her. She panicked and tried to run away from them but they were too fast for her.

Some of them jumped on Leigh's back and forced her down onto the ground. They then beat her up while she lay there. Leigh cried out in pain. They all laughed, looking down at her, and then just walked away. Young Sinead looked back still running and saw that no one had come to help Leigh. She was left there, crying.

Sinead found the memories so cruel. She stared at sleepyhead Cara. She felt so guilty, remembering that it was over twenty years ago:
Sinead and her younger brother were in their teens, visiting Leigh's family's house. Brandon looked terrified to see his big sister knocking at the front door. They looked at each other and gulped.
The front door opened. Leigh's mother came out. Her eyes were so swollen that they could tell she had been crying for a long time, possible for many hours.
"Sorry, madam. Are you okay?" Sinead asked, "We're here looking for Leigh."
Leigh's mother wailing was heartbreaking, "She's dead!"
Sinead opened her mouth in shock, she looked at her brother.
"Oh no…" Brandon whispered.

Sinead sighed; it did not make any sense. How could Leigh have been dead then, but now she's not? Sitting on the bed, tears rolled down her cheeks. She wiped them off and looked at the teardrops on her fingers.
Cara grunted in her sleep; she was trying to fight with herself to stop the nightmare from coming to get her. Sinead comforted her which woke her up.
"That's ok," she said.

"What's wrong?" Cara asked, touching the tears on Sinead's cheek before rubbing her own tired eyes. She was puzzled. "Hey, how did you get in?"

"Your window."

"But... I shut the -" Cara stopped herself, "Never mind. What's wrong? You look sad."

"Erm... I was haunted by old times."

"Of what?"

"You. I thought you... were dead. But... you're here, alive!"

Cara looked away, trying to avoid the conversation but Sinead forced her to look at her.

"You can tell me."

"My family tried to protect me from you all!" Cara snapped. She looked at Sinead's uncertain face. She grabbed the pen and paper to write it down and then walked out of the room. Sinead picked up the paper and read what Cara had just said to her.

Sinead sighed, "Fair enough."

Cara splashed her face with cold water at the bathroom sink. She then looked at herself in the mirror. She had a flashback in her mind of a teenage boy smirking back at her. She grunted and shook her head; she flinched as she tried to think of something else. She grabbed a towel to wipe the wet off her face and had a last look at herself before turning around. Sinead was already there which made Cara jump.

"Fuck! You made me shit myself! How long have you been standing there for?!"

"Long enough."

"But…?!" Cara looked at the mirror, then to herself. "Of course! Vampires and mirrors!" She exhaled and showed Sinead her fake smile, "Never mind."

Sinead pulled Cara close to her face and kissed her lips. It felt as though electric currents were shooting up inside Cara's body.

"Wait." Cara stopped her. She started to feel so light-headed. "Whoa."

Sinead worried about what would happen next.

Cara looked at Sinead's pale face until she reached for her blue-purple coloured lips. Cara came closer and touched her gently on her lips. Sinead told herself to be patient for Cara's next move.

"Your lips are so cold," signed Cara.

"I -" Sinead was stopped by Cara's index finger placed on her cold lips, shushing her. She watched as Cara moved to her face and gave her another kiss, and then a third until they couldn't let go of each other's lips. Cara pushed Sinead out of the bathroom; she kept pushing her until they reached Cara's bedroom.

Sinead took off her long-length jacket and her shirt.

Cara stepped backwards, her hands went over her head. She wasn't sure if she was ready.

Sinead froze, concerned. "Are you okay?"

Cara stared at Sinead's bra; she couldn't ignore her beautiful tits. Suddenly Rose's face popped up in her mind. Cara was breathless, crying. She was so uncertain about what she really wanted.

"Hey, hey, I'm sorry I shouldn't do this. I wasn't thinking," said Sinead, hugging Cara.

Cara hugged her so tightly and Sinead let her. "Shush…" Sinead continued to soothe Cara until she let her go to look up at her.

"I can't…" Cara murmured.

"Sure, I understand, that's fine." Sinead obeyed and she patiently picked up her shirt and jacket from the floor.

Cara cried, she felt so frustrated with herself.

"Hey, hey, that's alright." Sinead comforted her.

"No sex," Cara finally burst out. She reminded herself that Rose was the one who broke up the relationship so she was safe.

"No sex?" asked Sinead, wanting to make sure that she heard Cara's deaf voice correctly.

Cara nodded her head stiffly, she then grabbed the back of Sinead's neck and pulled her towards her face, lips-to-lips.

CHAPTER FIVE

Cara climbed over Rose's bed which interrupted Rose's sleep.

"Wha-" Cara clasped her fingers over Rose's lips to shush her. Rose was so surprised to see Cara on her bed and her heart was thumping so fast.

"I love you," said Cara in her deaf voice.

Finally. Rose was so relieved; it's what she had wanted to hear for the last two years.

"Of course, I love you too," signed Rose, unspoken.

Cara still had her hand over Rose's mouth while her other hand slid down into Rose's underwear. Rose moaned with pleasure. Cara decided to tease her so stopped touching. Rose looked at Cara.

"Why have you stopped?" said Rose, gutted. She watched as Cara opened her arms wide and pulled her t-shirt off. Rose bit her own lower lip, trying to control herself. *Beautiful*, she thought, as she looked at Cara's body.

Cara pulled off Rose's underwear and moved down there. Rose's eyes rolled backwards; she was enjoying every moment of it. She worked out that Cara had realised that sex was important and that she might try to save their relationship.

Suddenly a noise interrupted her pleasurable moment.

"What the hell's that noise?" Rose was puzzled as she looked down at Cara's eyes while she teased around Rose's pussy.

Again, the noise annoyed her.

Rose woke from her sleep. She groaned, realising that it was just a dream. Her *wish* dream. Suddenly she heard a noise and realised that it wasn't part of her dream. She stared at the bedroom door. There were no sounds of footsteps. The door blew open and Yves stood in the hallway, looking at Rose and smiling.

"Help!!" Rose shrieked.

"I think you need to chill," Yves said.

But it didn't stop her screaming. She ran to the window and opened it.

"Fair enough." Yves sighed; he hadn't expected how it would turn out. He zoomed towards Rose and pinned her to the floor.

This shocked Rose. She tried to push him off but it was impossible; he was just too strong. Rose screamed for her life. Yves opened his mouth wide, revealing fangs, which horrified her.

Her screams became louder and then turned into shrieking.

CHAPTER SIX

Sinead sat beside Cara's side, she was naked except for her underwear. She watched Cara in her sleep, who was also just in her boxers. Sinead got a flashback, she was at her secondary school, in the gym hall. Sinead and Leigh were teenagers; it was their first time making love in the changing room. They enjoyed each other all night long, exploring as many different sexual positions as they could find. The next day, they put their school uniforms back on before the janitor unlocked the door. He apologised for accidently locking them in overnight. Their parents hugged them both, so relieved that they were okay. Leigh and Sinead looked into each other's eyes before being sent home with a day off school.

Unfortunately, the next day was the weekend that Sinead was told that Leigh was dead.

Sinead sighed, she wished she could go back and change the past but it was too late and she knew it. No one can go back and fix the past. Her thoughts were suddenly interrupted by Cara's mobile alarm, vibrating under her pillow. Cara woke up, grabbed her mobile, and switched it off. She rubbed her eyes and saw Sinead sat there so she screamed out in fright which made Sinead jumpy as well.

"Shit! - you scared me!" said Cara breathlessly. She put her hand on her chest and could feel her heart thumping so fast that it felt as though it was about to jump out of her ribcage. Then she frowned, "What are you doing here in the morning?"

"I have nowhere to stay," said Sinead using sign language which was improving a bit but she was sheepish, "So... I just wondered if... can I stay here, through the sunlight days?"

"But, what about your home?"

"Yeah, well... it's difficult. You see, I'm sharing with someone else."

"Ah, you're afraid that 'someone' might do something bad to you?"

Sinead shrugged. Cara sighed, she didn't like to share her house with anyone since she fell out with her past flatmates.

"Fine. But promise me - "

"No, no bites or fangs, I promised." Sinead confirmed, already having obeyed her.

Cara sighed, she accepted that it was a big challenge and Sinead had promised.

"Look, I'm so sorry. The past - what I did... I mean, what *we* did to you."

"Shit happens."

"Hmm." Sinead paused, "So... C-A-R-A or L-E-I-G-H?"

Cara looked away once Sinead had fingerspelled 'Leigh'. Sinead came close to Cara, clasping her cheeks. Cara's eyes looked away to avoid eye contact until Sinead got her to look at her. Their eyes meet.

"I... I don't want to talk about it," Cara said. She knew what Sinead was going to say.

After Cara said that, Sinead stopped herself from saying anything more.

"I have to go," Cara spoke to break the silence.

"What time are you coming back?" Sinead asked.

That. That was exactly why Cara didn't like sharing a home with anyone. She sighed, "After two."

"Ok, I'll wait for you."

"Stay away from the sun. I don't want to see ashes everywhere when I come back," Cara mimed.

"Don't worry, I know what I'm doing." Sinead smiled.

"Okay, whatever." Cara rolled her eyes and left. Sinead let out a small laugh.

* * * * *

Cara pulled several envelopes from the mailroom shelves when, out of the corner of her eye, she saw her boss approach.

"Oh, great(!)" She mouthed to herself.

The boss stood next to her. She noticed that his face looked like he'd just seen a ghost or something, or that possibly he had some *very* bad news.

Cara was puzzled; she'd never seen him like that before. "What?"

"Cara… erm… police… here.. to see… you." Her boss pointed at two police officers who were standing at the back of the mailroom.

Cara saw them whispering to each other, "What have I done?" she said, looking at her boss with confusion.

The boss rubbed his hands against his hips as he struggled to find the right words to tell her, "Ah…"

"What is it?" Cara tried to encourage him to speak up. Her boss gulped. "What?!" Cara signed without using her voice.

"Rose." The boss finally blurted out the word by attempting to sign 'flower' but from his nose so it looked more like the sign for 'tissue paper'. Cara, however, caught his lip pattern: 'Rose'.

"…Well?"

"Police… thinking… Rose…" continued her boss but again, using the wrong sign for 'Rose', "was murdered."

The boss made the signs for 'choking' and 'dead' to Cara, who was now so shocked. He then signed "And body… gone."

Tears filled Cara's eyes when she realised that something had happened to Rose. *Please not Rose*, she thought.

One of the police officers arrived to arrest Cara, "Sorry," he said as he forced her hands behind her back and clicked the handcuffs on her.

"You better get her an interpreter," her boss warned them before he looked at her and said, "That's ok, they just want to talk to you."

Cara was too shocked to speak.

* * * * *

Sinead lay on Cara's bed, she felt so bored as she pressed the remote control buttons to change the channels on the small television. She gave up deciding what to watch so just left the news on the screen.

"Rose Lynch's body has gone missing under suspicious circumstances. She is believed to have been murdered. Cara Miles, a Royal Mail postal worker, has been arrested at her workplace in connection with the case, enquiries are still ongoing." The newsreader spoke on the television which had captions automatically on the screen.

"Oh, shit!" Sinead was shocked, quickly dialling numbers on the mobile phone which Cara usually left behind whenever she went to work.

The phone rang in Brandon's office at the police station. He sighed before answering it, "Brandon Goodwin speaking." His voice sounded so annoyed. All he wanted to do was to focus on his work without being disturbed. As he listened to the voice on the other end of the line his eyes widened with surprise.

"Sinead?! Where have -?!"

"Brandon! Listen to me, let me explain first. Leigh - I mean Cara Miles, was with me last night. She has absolutely nothing to do with Rose's disappearance or murder," Sinead explained.

"Actually, she *was* with her last night, at the carnival. However, witnesses have confirmed that at ten o'clock Miles left, by herself. Lynch's neighbours mentioned that they heard screaming coming from her house at around one o'clock in the morning."

"I was with Miles all night, from midnight onwards."

"Okay, I have to add that to the report."

"So, where is she?"

"We have sent her home but she's not allowed to leave the country; she may be called back in to be interviewed for further information at a later stage."

"What time did you let her go?"

"She left at noon-ish so she should be home by now."

Sinead looked at the clock: 3.23pm, "She isn't home."

"How do you know?"

"Because I'm still at her house." Sinead looked out of the window - sunlight. She sighed, "Thank you, bro," she said and hung up.

"Sin -" Brandon looked at his phone with confusion.

* * * * *

Cara walked down the road in the dark, very drunk. She had been in the pub all day long, drowning in alcohol after she had been given the shocking news. She saw someone peering out their bedroom window.

"What?!" Cara shouted as she shrugged her shoulders and gave them a 'rough' look to make the nosey person stop peering out and shut their curtains. "Fuck you…" She started to cry. Her legs wobbled until her knees gave way and she fell to the ground. She sobbed loudly.

ZOOM!

Someone grabbed her off the ground at a high speed. Cara couldn't scream as that 'someone' had covered her mouth which terrified her.

Cara was dropped on the footpath outside her house. She turned around to see who it was.

"OH FUCK YOU!" She shouted.

Enraged, Sinead's fangs appeared.

Cara fell back on her doorstep and froze in terror.

"Are you crazy? You go out all day and night?! Aren't you aware that vampires are out there at night time?! What if they found you and you would become their next victim?!" Sinead snarled.

Cara didn't pick up what Sinead was saying. She had held her breath for too long, terrified to move, or even breathe. Sinead had forgotten about Cara's phobia. Her fangs disappeared back into her teeth. Finally, Cara was able to breathe again.

"I'm sorry," Sinead comforted her, "I'm just worried that vampires might catch you before I do."

"Rose…" whimpered Cara before bursting into tears, "Rose… She's gone!"

Sinead pulled Cara towards her and hugged her, "Shhh…" she hushed.

CHAPTER SEVEN

Cara refused to sleep, she refused to drink, even when Sinead offered her a glass of water or a cup of tea. All she did was cry, continually, and walk around the living room with a bottle of vodka in her hand. She became heavily drunk and was still swallowing the alcohol down her throat with large gulps.

"Please... just stop," Sinead begged.

"It's my fault!" Cara cried.

Sinead managed to pick up Cara's voice and, with her head shaking, said "No, it wasn't your fault!"

"Yes, it is! We had just broken up and now she's deeeead!" Cara scowled.

Sinead was taken by surprise, realising that Cara had a girlfriend she didn't know about. *They broke up? Was it because we kissed? No, impossible. It must have happened before Cara kissed me.*

Cara's anger was building up inside her. She realised something before looking at Sinead, "Wait a minute...!"

Sinead caught Cara before she lost her balance.

"It's you. It's your fault." Cara pointed at Sinead's shoulder, she didn't know if she had hurt Sinead or not but she didn't give a fuck.

Sinead didn't say anything. She let Cara get it off her chest; she knew it was just the drink talking.

"You... Cold... BLOOD!" shouted Cara as she pointed at the vein in her forearm.

"Cold-blood?" Sinead double-checked what Cara had just said.

"Yes! You… kill… people… for blood!"

"Whoa, wait - that's totally different."

"Murder… suck blood… difference?! Pfft!" scoffed Cara as she poured more vodka down her throat.

Suddenly, Sinead used her powers to force the bottle out of Cara's hand and smashed it against the wall. Cara looked at the broken bottle, horrified.

"That's… my… last… one!"

"I stopped sucking people's blood since I re-met you."

"Oh, so it's my fault you go to see blood-alcohol counselling(!) A few days ago you were close to killing me!" Cara scoffed, "Nothing would have happened if you'd never come back into my life!"

Sinead slowly walked backwards when she realised that Cara might be right. She turned up in her life and had already fucked it up for her again.

Cara was puzzled; she wondered what Sinead was doing.

Sinead turned towards the front door.

Cara, quickly realising it was early morning and the sun was rising outside, shouted, "NO!!"

Sinead took a step outside the house. She immediately felt an intense burning pain. Smoke began to escape from her skin. Cara ran out and pushed Sinead back into the house before the sun rays killed her.

Cara breathlessly slammed the door shut. She slowly turned her head to look at Sinead's unconscious body.

Sinead's face had been so badly burned that some of the flesh had completely burnt away, showing part of her skull. Cara knew she was about to throw up because she could feel the vomit rising in her throat. She had just enough time to rush into the kitchen before violently retching down the sink. She retched continually until she could see stars in front of her eyes, fell on the kitchen floor and blacked out.

* * * * *

Cara was asleep, whimpering and soaked in sweat. She had a cold, wet hand towel placed on her forehead. She opened her eyes and looked up, seeing Sinead. Sinead's face was pale but back to normal.

"Sinead!" Cara jumped and hugged Sinead, "I'm so sorry!" she cried. Sinead hugged her, squeezing her tightly. "Sinead…" whispered Cara. They let go of each other to be able to have eye contact. "Please… don't ever do that again."

Sinead understood and nodded.

"Never again," repeated Cara.

"I won't." Sinead promised.

They looked at each other for a bit longer until Cara began sobbing softly and leant her head on Sinead's chest.

Another hour had passed and Cara couldn't sleep, she was still grieving over Rose's disappearance or death. This worried Sinead; she tried to feed her and encouraged her to drink some water but she wouldn't.

"Please try to get some sleep," begged Sinead. Cara stared out blankly, not even blinking once. Sinead sighed, she felt she had no choice but to put her hand in front of Cara's face. Within two seconds, Cara was asleep. She also made sure that Cara wouldn't have any bad dreams throughout the night. Sinead kissed Cara's forehead.

"Goodnight," she whispered and left Cara sleeping peacefully.

* * * * *

Sinead arrived at the footpath in front of Rose's house and saw the police tape that cordoned off the front door; the house was now a possible murder crime scene. She bent to walk under the police tape and entered the house. She looked around, searching for clues until she reached Rose's bedroom. As she walked in, she noticed blood on the floor beside the window. She sniffed and immediately recognised the smell. She had a sense that something was not right and then left.

* * * * *

Meanwhile, back at Cara's house, a figure flew straight towards her bedroom window, opened it, and went in. The figure stood and watched Cara in her sleep, and then their footsteps crept slowly towards the bed. A pale hand reached over and touched Cara's hair to wake her up.

Cara winced as she struggled to open her eyes; she was so hung-over. She looked up at the figure and squinted her eyes, trying hard to focus her blurred vision to see who was standing there.

"Rose!" Cara gasped, quickly hugging her then letting go. "Everyone thought you were…"

She stopped mid-sentence because she noticed Rose's very pale skin tone. She knew then that Rose had become a vampire.

"No…" whimpered Cara. She fell off the bed and crawled backwards in terror.

Rose followed her.

"Please don't!" Cara begged, "I don't want to become like you!"

"You've no choice."

It terrified her. She tried to escape out of the door but Rose used her powers to slam it shut. Rose followed Cara wherever she crawled until Rose lost her patience and jumped towards Cara.

Cara managed to get away before Rose caught her and snarled.

Cara grabbed her only chair and threw it at Rose but it was pointless. Rose used her power again, the chair was blown against the wall and was smashed to pieces.

"Oh, shit!" Cara whispered, seeing Rose quickly coming towards her. Cara flinched, she ran and grabbed any objects that she could and threw them at Rose. One by one each object was destroyed by Rose's power; not a single item hit her face or body. Rose suddenly flew at Cara and pushed her down on the floor. Cara got up quickly and hit Rose to defend herself. But Rose was too strong and too fast for Cara to fight back. With Cara's heavy hangover, it was simply hopeless. Rose kicked Cara in the face, strong enough to send Cara's whole body twirling through the air before landing hard on the floor. Cara groaned, she wished she'd never drank so much as her headache felt even worse than having a migraine.

Rose zoomed over to where Cara lay and continued to kick her in the face and stomach. Cara screamed out in pain and started to cough up blood. Her body became too weak to fight back. Rose turned Cara's body over onto her back and sat on top of her, pinning her legs to the floor with her own. Cara stared up at Rose as Rose pulled her head towards her, with her mouth wide open and fangs showing.

Cara froze with fear.

Rose bit into Cara's neck and started to suck out her blood.

Cara was now too weak to scream but her eyes clearly showed that she was in terrible pain. She gasped silently.

Rose stopped, and gave a satisfied gasp.

Cara saw her blood all over Rose's mouth.

"Yummy," Rose smiled, licking the blood from her lips.

Cara started to feel her body becoming numb. Her vision blurred and then she blacked out.

Rose dumped Cara's body down on the floor. She stood and looked over at the window. Yves invited himself in and stood on the floor; he saw Cara's body lying on the floor.

"Bravo, Rose, excellent work." Yves was impressed, he bent down and ran his fingers over Cara's unconscious face.

"Why didn't Sinead bite her?" asked Rose, still enjoying the taste of Cara's blood on her lips.

"Don't know. Maybe your girlfriend brainwashed her," Yves guessed.

"Ex," snapped Rose.

"Pardon?"

"Cara was my ex-girlfriend," Rose added.

Yves realised that he couldn't comment on that, "We gotta go."

"What about her?"

"Nah, let's leave her here… I want Sinead to see it all. Anyway, you'd better clean it up in here." Yves looked around at the messy room, then left.

Rose looked around and sighed, wishing she'd never made the room this messy in the first place.

CHAPTER EIGHT

Brandon had fallen asleep at his office desk. He was exhausted from working at the police station all night, focussing on the murder investigation.

"Brandon?" The voice woke Brandon up, he looked up to make sure that it was Sinead. It was.

"Sinead! Where have you been?! Come here!" said Brandon and hugged his big sister.

"Well, you wouldn't believe me if I told you." Sinead sighed and glanced over at Brandon's paperwork. "What case are you working on?"

"Are you okay? You look so pale."

"You didn't answer my question," said Sinead bluntly, avoiding the subject of her skin colour.

"Sorry, um... I'm working on an unsolved disappearance/murder case at the Lynch's."

"Hmm." Sinead looked around for a seat to sit down on. "Explain," she said as she brought a chair to sit beside him at the desk.

Brandon sat down behind his desk looking puzzled, "Are you working on this case as well?"

"No, not really... She's a friend of mine... a friend. Go on." Sinead almost stopped herself saying the word 'friend' because she wasn't sure if she was an enemy or a friend of Cara at the moment.

"Well, it's like I told you on the phone yesterday afternoon. However, a new member of the public has now come forward stating that they witnessed both Lynch and

Miles on the evening of the disappearance. They were standing in a queue, possibly arguing, outside the carnival circus tent. Miles then left, alone."

"They broke up that night, I believe."

"How...?" Brandon asked, puzzled.

"I just figured it out. Go on."

"Well, we found a set of footprints at the crime scene, but strangely they were only present from the hallway to Lynch's bedroom door and in the bedroom itself. And no other DNA has been found except Lynch's. The suspect's footprint boot size is eleven so it had to be a male's."

"The footprints were only found in the hallway outside of Lynch's bedroom and inside her room?"

"Yes, only upstairs, there were no footprints detected anywhere else in the property."

"Hmm. I reckon I know who did this," Sinead said.

"You do? Well, who did it?"

"Yves."

"Who?"

"A vampire."

"A vampire?" Brandon let out a huge laugh, "It can't be! Vampires don't actually exist, Sinead, it's just a myth."

"Who told you that?" said Sinead with one of her eyebrows raised.

"I'm serious." Brandon was getting really annoyed with his sister's teasing.

"Uh-huh, so am I."

"Ok, tell me how you know that 'Yves' is a vampire?"

"Because he bit me."

"...What?"

"So I'm now one of them."

Brandon rolled his eyes; he'd just about lost his patience with her. "Look, I'm not in the mood for your shit."

Sinead suddenly showed Brandon her fangs which gave him such a fright that he fell off his chair.

"I did say you wouldn't believe me if I told you. So there you go, you can believe it now."

Brandon crawled backwards on the floor and bumped his head against the wall. He covered his neck to protect himself from her fangs.

It hurt Sinead too much to see him like that, "Brandon, relax. I'm not going to bite you." Her fangs disappeared back into her teeth.

Brandon was still shaking, fearing for his life.

"I'm not going to hurt you. I just want to help you solve this case." Sinead pointed at the case files on the desk then sighed, bending herself back on the chair, "I gave up sucking humans' blood five nights ago."

"W-w-when did you, um, become, like them?" Brandon stuttered.

"Over three weeks ago, it happened back in the Gay Village," answered Sinead, which triggered her to have a flashback of the gang of vampires who had attacked her.

"Shit... that explains why you didn't turn up for work."

"Yeah. I miss my life. My new normal life is that I won't see daylight ever again," Sinead said in sorrow.

Brandon let go of his neck. "Um... How can you manage to stay 'alive' without sucking people's blood?"

"Animals. Obviously, vegan people won't be happy to hear that." Sinead actually felt so bad doing it but she had to keep herself 'alive'.

"Ew. What's changed your mind?"

"I had no choice; they decided to attack me so I ended up just like them!" Sinead snapped, then calmed herself down, "I'm sorry…"

"That's alright," Brandon quickly replied but still kept his distance from her.

"It's just that I sucked one or two people's blood every night until I met Leigh."

"Leigh? As in Leigh Smith?" Brandon was puzzled.

Sinead stared at him for a few seconds before nodding.

"Was she the one that we… bullied at school?"

"I'm afraid so." Sinead knew that she, her brother, Bob, and Jason all felt so guilty about what they had done to Leigh all those years ago.

"B-b-but she was dead!"

"That's what her parents made us believe… but she isn't. Maybe… I don't know… they moved away to start a fresh new life and to get away from all of us. Brandon, you've re-met Leigh."

"Did I?"

"Mmm," said Sinead who went on to explain, "Leigh changed her name to Cara Miles."

"Cara? Is Lynch's girlfriend? I mean, ex… Are you telling me that it was her that we interviewed yesterday morning?" Brandon was dumbfounded. Sinead nodded again. Brandon scratched his head and said, "What are we supposed to tell them?" He lifting the disappearance/murder case files. "This." He dropped the files on the desk again, "And you?"

"You can't, Brandon. You just can't... Vampires are too powerful for our team to attack. So... just say nothing, not yet." Sinead explained, zooming towards the door and turning her head, "Let me handle this."

"How do you do that?!" exclaimed Brandon. Sinead had heard the phrase *'How do you do that?!'* quite often; it was nothing new.

"Magic." Sinead opened the door on her way out.

"Where are you going?!" Brandon yelled out.

"To protect Leigh." Brandon heard Sinead's response before she shut the office door.

"Phew," he exhaled. He really didn't expect anything like that to happen that night.

CHAPTER NINE

Cara was asleep, not moving. Her bedroom was now clean and tidy. The chair which had been smashed to pieces was now back to normal; the same old chair. All of the objects which Cara threw at Rose earlier were now back where they were before. There wasn't a single drop of blood where Cara had been bleeding from when Rose attacked her. Everything looked as if nothing at all had happened.

Sinead arrived through the bedroom window, she approached the bed and smiled gently, so relieved to see Cara still in her bed. She climbed onto the bed and kissed Cara's forehead. Sinead frowned, "You're not warm..." She sniffed the air and recognised the smell, "...Shit!" She pulled the duvet off the bed and saw Cara's whole body - a very pale skin tone, matching her own. She then noticed two small, purplish-red circles on Cara's neck. "NO!!" Sinead grunted.

Cara turned over in her semi-conscious state, moaning very weakly.

"YVES!!" Sinead yelled, turning towards the window but then quickly backing away as she saw the sunrise. "Damnit!" Using her power, she furiously raised her arms and quickly clapped her hands together which caused the curtains to shut tightly by themselves. She dropped to her knees and punched her fists against the floor, grunting because she just couldn't believe it. Yves had actually been following her over the past few days. She wished she'd thought of this before.

Cara groaned which made Sinead stop her punching and instead she got back on the bed to get closer to Cara. Cara moaned as Sinead gently pulled her close to her side. Sinead cried.

"Rose... please, no...!" murmured Cara. She was reliving the fight between Rose and herself in a nightmare. It was at that moment that Sinead realised that it was Rose who had attacked Cara.

Yves must have encouraged her, she thought, quietly sobbing, "I'm so sorry that I have failed you…"

* * * * *

As the sky turned into darkness, Sinead woke up and noticed that the other side of Cara's bed was empty.

"Leigh!" She panicked, zooming out of the bedroom window, fearing for Cara's, rather Leigh's, safety. Sinead had a bad habit of calling her Leigh.

Cara's walking was so wobbly; she was frightened of everything that surrounded her. She was so confused and completely lost. She had never felt anything as different as this before and she couldn't remember how it happened. The last thing she remembered was being in the pub, drinking too much, just after she was released from the police station. The news of Rose's disappearance, or possibly death, had hit her big time.

Rose? Did I see Rose? She thought. She shook her head as her thoughts were just making her even more confused and right now she didn't know where she was or why her body felt *so* different. She couldn't tell if she was still *drunk* from the other night. Her legs began to give away, she fell on the ground, banging her head, and blacked out.

CHAPTER TEN

Cara slowly opened her eyes, moaning. Her skin had turned a greyish pale colour, she had no energy left in her body and wasn't feeling too good. She turned her neck to one side and realised how painful it was, similar to when she'd caught the flu a few nights before. She looked at one of her wrists and then the other; both were restrained in metal cuffs that were attached to chains hung from a rock-wall. She looked from side to side, she was being held in some kind of big circular area, somewhere underground by the looks of it. She searched around the area where she was being held prisoner; it reminded her of the old abandoned mine. She remembered studying the history of the old mine. Suddenly she saw something which terrified her; some of the vampires were asleep, hanging upside-down from the ceiling of the abandoned mine. Cara wanted to scream but she was too weak to do so.

Rose turned up, her smiling looked so inhumane. Seeing her face triggered Cara's memory of her violent attack; she knew then that it was Rose who'd attacked her in her bedroom.

"You?" Cara whimpered.

She turned her face away when Rose came closer to her. Rose grabbed Cara's chin which hurt her and forced her to face Rose. Rose then forced her mouth against Cara's lips. Cara tried to stop her but Rose was too strong and Cara too weak to resist her, there was nothing she could do. Rose gave Cara a passionate kiss as her punishment. Cara's crying was muffled by Rose's tongue which she'd shoved inside her mouth. She could feel Rose's hand pushing down into her pants. She desperately tried to shout 'Stop!' but no sound escaped from her throat as Rose had completely blocked her mouth.

Rose's fingers touched Cara's clit and she started rubbing it. Cara gasped in her discomfort as Rose let go of her mouth. Rose kept teasing all over Cara's pussy with her fingers; she didn't care that Cara hated it. Cara cried out and moaned because it was so uncomfortable. Rose put her fingers inside Cara's vagina.

"No...!" Cara wailed as she banged her head hard against the rock wall and her eyes kept rolling back in her head with her pain and confusion.

Rose furiously fucked her with her fingers. She didn't realise but at that moment, Cara was experiencing a really traumatic flashback. Rose pulled her wet fingers out of Cara's pussy and quickly grabbed her chin using the same hand. Cara was terrified.

"You've fucked Sinead, haven't you?! Was it her you fucked behind my back?!"

Cara was too weak to answer but just managed to shake her head slightly.

"LIAR!" screamed Rose, squeezing Cara's jaws so tightly that it made her wince. Rose used her free hand to whack Cara across her face and she groaned.

"That's enough," Yves said, as he appeared out of nowhere, standing behind Rose and tightly grasping her wrist. She yanked it to try and free herself from his grip.

Yves lifted Cara's chin and had a look, "Give me the bowl," he said.

Rose laughed, picking up the bowl which was already full of blood. She couldn't wait to see Cara become a pure vampire, then she would be hers for good.

Yves forced Cara to open her mouth wide before pouring the blood into her mouth. She tried to spit it out but Yves clenched her jaw tightly shut to stop her. Cara was trying not to swallow the blood but Yves noticed this so he raised his hand and used his power on her throat. Cara's eyes widened as she realised that she couldn't hold on any longer, she swallowed the mouthful of blood. She started coughing and spluttering and she cried as Yves poured even more blood into her mouth and forced her to swallow it until, eventually, there was no blood left in the bowl.

"All done," said Yves, satisfied.

As the blood flowed down Cara's throat and spread throughout her body, her own blood cells started to reject and fight against the new and different blood cells inside her. This made her feel so groggy, so confused, and was deeply painful. Her body trembled and the pain became so unbearable that she screamed out, waking the upside-down sleepyhead vampires.

Yves looked wary and uncertain as he watched Cara's reaction to drinking the blood.

"What the hell's the matter with her?" Rose said, anxiously looking on.

"I don't know... Never seen anything like this, ever," Yves replied. Rose couldn't stand watching Cara's continual screaming.

Eventually, Cara's eyes rolled back, her head bent down forwards and her body ceased shaking.

Yves frowned; he wondered what effects this would have on her body. In the past, most of the humans that they had turned into vampires were changed within just a day. With Cara, however, a day had already passed but there was still no sign of any change to her body.

His ear picked up noise from far away.

"Someone's coming," Yves said as he walked away which confused Rose because she didn't hear a thing.

Inside the long tunnel cave, a few vampires walked out of the old mine and into the dark night; they were heading for the city. They just missed Sinead sneaking into the mine. She walked and then zoomed down to the other end of the long tunnel which was the entrance to the large circular area, where Cara was being kept prisoner.

Sinead immediately saw Cara chained to the rock-wall with her head bent down; she zoomed over to her and carefully lifted her chin upwards.

"Leigh? Are you alright?" Sinead could tell that Cara was still dazed.

"Well, well, well - look who's here!" Yves' voice came from behind Sinead.

Sinead turned and saw Yves sat on the chair made of stones before getting up and walking along with his arms open wide.

"What have you done to her?!" Sinead roared.

"We treated her like a baby; we blood-fed her and we hope she'll grow up quickly to become like the rest of us, of course." Yves looked at Rose walking towards him and smiling, "Meet Cara's ex-girlfriend, Rose."

"Hello, you must be Sinead who no one told me about." Rose looked her up and down, it was no wonder that Cara went after her instead of herself. She felt full of jealously and anger all at once.

"Why did you do that to her, and her?!" Sinead shouted with her finger pointed to Cara then Rose.

"Well, Sinead… you know rule number one… there are no rules!" Yves exclaimed dramatically. "We have our own freedom. We spot humans, grab them, then we either kill them or make them become one of us. No one's going to stop us. So then, Sinead, we were wondering; why didn't you suck Cara's blood?"

"Because she doesn't want to become one and I respect that!" Sinead snapped back at Yves.

"Well, everyone said that before they turn into one," Yves scoffed and turned to Rose to ask her, "Did you complain?"

"Not a bit," Rose smiled.

"But Leigh's so different!"

"Cara is her name!" Rose corrected her.

"*'Cara'* hates vampires!"

Rose flinched.

"Well, she's a soon-to-be-vampire... and you are, of course, a vampire too. Is there a problem?" Yves added.

"I've told you - she does not want to become a vampire!" Sinead repeated.

"She'll change her mind once she's fully recovered," said Rose.

"Sinead, my friend, you have to accept the vampire world; we do whatever we want. Cara is already dead, here with us."

"You fuck-!" Sinead started yelling at Yves but the three vampires immediately zoomed over and grabbed her before she had a chance to attack him. "Lemme go!" She grunted.

They forced her against the rock-wall and put her wrists in metal cuffs to restrain her.

Sinead looked over at Cara who was still unconscious.

Yves came closer to her and laid his finger on Cara's cheek.

"At dawn, I will ask you to make your own decision. So, you have to wait here and babysit this girl", said Yves before he turned away, followed by the group of vampires as they left the old mine.

Rose looked at Sinead and Cara; she didn't trust leaving Cara alone with Sinead.

"Rose!" It was Yves calling out her name.

Rose, grunting and furiously, stared at Sinead and pointed her finger at Cara. "She's mine," she warned her while she stepped backwards, as if she had no choice but to join the rest of the group.

Sinead looked up at one of her cuffed wrists and tried to wiggle it free from the restraint but it was impossible. She then tried to use her new powers to break free but that was also hopeless. She hit the back of her head against the rock wall in frustration, "FUCK!" she grunted.

CHAPTER ELEVEN

Yves, Rose, and the rest of the vampires arrived outside one of the city's nightclubs.

"Ugh, heterosexual nightclub; I hate straight people," complained Rose.

"Just pretend that they're homosexual." Yves' response was blunt as he walked along with his group of vampires. Rose rolled her eyes, following on behind them.

Two bouncers stood in front of the nightclub entrance. The group of vampires went inside but Yves and Rose stayed outside to chat with the bouncers.

Rose got one of the bouncer's attention by giving him a sexy smile, "Wanna fuck?" she suggested, uninterested.

"Sure, babe," replied the bouncer, following her into a nearby alleyway.

"Tell me, how much is your salary working here?" Yves asked the other bouncer.

"Why do you ask?" The bouncer replied to Yves without making any eye contact with him or moving from his upright position.

"That's the kinda job I'm looking for, y'know?" answered Yves.

The bouncer turned to look Yves up and down before looking ahead again, "I don't reckon it would suit you."

Yves laughed lightly whilst rubbing his narrow beard, "Black belt in Taekwondo."

The bouncer found this so impressive, "Well, it depends. This nightclub's very popular, so -"

The bouncer's speech was interrupted when he heard the sound of screaming coming from down the alleyway. Suddenly Yves bit his neck and sucked out his blood until he collapsed on the ground, dead. Yves looked up at Rose coming out of the alleyway.

"He's disgusting, but his blood tasted lush." Rose wiped the blood off her lips with tissue paper and threw it away.

Yves smiled with relief and pride; he was confident that this time he'd made the right choice to turn Rose into a vampire. He wiped the blood from his mouth before they entered the nightclub.

There was loud screaming coming from various victims inside the nightclub where the vampires were attacking them.

CHAPTER TWELVE

Sinead stared at the ground feeling furious; she had been waiting impatiently for several hours, until finally she heard a groaning sound.

Cara opened her eyes; her energy was becoming a bit stronger but she was still very groggy. She blinked her eyes several times, trying to get a clear vision but her mind was still so confused and she was in a lot of pain. Sinead tried to get her attention but Cara was too focused on trying to free her wrists from the cuffs. She couldn't see Sinead because she was almost blind. All she wanted to do was to get her wrists free so that she could rub her face to rid herself of the pain.

"Cooee! Look who's awake this morning!" Yves exclaimed.

Sinead watched as Yves, Rose and the others entered with their faces and long-length jackets covered in blood.

As soon as Cara's vision became clearer she saw Rose. Her anger was finally showing as she struggled again to get her wrists out of their cuffs.

"What are you trying to say?" Yves encouraged Cara to talk but Rose clasped his shoulder.

"She can't hear you, but don't you understand her body language?" Rose continued, smiling because she was looking forward to what would happen next, "She wants to fight with *me*."

"Indeed?" Yves met Rose's eyes. Rose nodded. "Good." He then turned and nodded at some of the vampire group, giving them an order.

"What are you doing?" said Rose and Sinead at the same time.

Yves smiled and replied, "Watch and learn." He turned back to the others and instructed them, "Let her go, no biting ok?"

Two of the vampires went towards Cara.

Rose quickly moved to try to protect her but Yves pulled her backwards and said, "Rose, back off."

"It's me she wants!" Rose shouted desperately but Yves just ignored her. "Yves!"

"Leave her alone!" Sinead grunted, she wanted to stop them but her wrists were tightly locked in metal cuffs. She could only watch what they were going to do to Cara.

Yves raised his hands and used his power to unlock Cara's cuffs.

Cara fell to the ground, breathless and trembling. It was the blood that she'd been forced to drink which made her body tremble.

She grunted, forcing herself to build up her energy before looking up at Rose.

Rose tried to stand in front to face Cara but Yves still held her back.

Cara stared at Rose; her eyes were swirls of black and white all over. She suddenly started screeching and ran towards Rose but was pushed by another vampire into the surrounding crowd. They all started to attack her. Cara punched and kicked them to try and get them out of her way so that she could face Rose, but they were too strong for her. She cried out in pain as each vampire took turns to punch and kick her. She fell to the ground but the vampires just continued to attack her, hurting her all over her body. Cara realised that she couldn't fight back, she was crying and moaning in agony.

Sinead grew more and more worried about Cara.

Rose was really shocked; she had expected that Cara would be strong by now but she wasn't.

"Alright, that's enough," Yves told the vampire group to stop their violence, "Bring her to me."

Two of them brought Cara over to Yves. Cara's body was limp and numb; she had given up the fight.

"Oh, you poor thing," said Yves with a fake soothing tone as he hugged her.

As he held her close, Cara could see Yves' neck really clearly.

Sinead saw Cara gazing at his neck, as did Rose.

Cara was so tempted, she opened her mouth and her fangs slowly began to grow downwards. She wailed with the pain; it hurt so much to have fangs come out of her normal teeth.

"Leigh…" Sinead whispered.

Cara's eyes suddenly changed back to normal; she blinked and looked down at Yves' neck. She realised that this was exactly what they were trying to get her into so she turned away.

Sinead sighed, so relieved.

Yves wasn't however, he was furious. He used just one hand to push Cara away; it sent her body flying backwards through the air until it slammed against the rock-wall and she fell to the ground. She just lay there, not moving.

"Put her back." Yves nodded his head to order the vampires to lift Cara and put her back in the chained cuffs before Yves used his power to lock them. He walked over to her and lifted her chin to face him. Cara whimpered with panic; she felt so groggy and her body ached so much that it felt as though she had been badly burned.

"Now you should go to sleep." Yves raised his hand again which forced Cara to close her eyes and knocked her out. "Ok, Sinead, you have to make your decision," he said with his fingers resting on Cara's face, "If you want her to stay a vampire then you must force her to suck your blood. Or, if you refuse, one of us will kill her for you."

Sinead was wide-eyed in horror.

"No!" shouted Rose as she zoomed to Cara's side to try and protect her.

Yves ignored her and continued, "Well?"

Sinead looked at Cara. Cara's head was bent down and she just looked fucked. Sinead knew that she had let her down. She'd failed to stop Cara from becoming the one thing she loathed most - a vampire. Sinead exhaled deeply through her nose and replied, "I have another option in my mind."

"Go on."

"I choose dawn," Sinead said seriously.

Yves wasn't pleased to hear that; he raised his hands in fury.

Suddenly Sinead's wrists were freed from her cuffs; she tried to walk past Yves but he stopped her and asked, "What would you like me to do with Cara?"

Sinead looked at Yves calmly but inside she was scared that something would happen to her Leigh. "It's your decision," she replied, hoping that he wouldn't listen to her. She forced herself to walk out of the area.

Yves turned away to cover his angry face from the rest of his vampires.

"Please..." Rose begged him as she wrapped herself around sleeping Cara; she feared for Cara's safety.

Sinead walked alone and in sorrow through the long tunnel. She experienced a flashback of herself and Cara sat on Cara's bed in her house.

"Please... don't ever do that again." Cara was breathless and drunk, "Never again."

Tears ran down Sinead's cheeks. Looking up, she could see the early morning sky at the end of the tunnel.

Yves, Rose and everyone in the large circular area stood waiting. Suddenly they heard a screaming echo and then an explosion in the distance. Rose jumped with fright on hearing that for the very first time.

Yves closed his eyes, disappointed that he had chosen the wrong person to become a vampire.

"Yves..." whimpered Rose to get his attention, "Please don't kill my Cara."

Yves went straight towards Cara which made Rose shriek with panic. Yves used his power to wake Cara up.

"Don't you dare!" Rose tried to fight him off but one of the vampires used their strong arms to pull her back by her waist.

"Shush," Yves hushed Rose before turning back to face Cara. Rose was sobbing; she didn't want Yves to touch Cara. "I'm not going to kill her," Yves finally mentioned making Rose stop struggling against the vampire's hold.

"Let me go you bastard!" Rose shouted at the vampire to let her go of her waist.

Cara's eyes kept rolling back inside her head and she was moaning continually. She couldn't see a thing. She felt as though she had fallen into a nettle bush and had a billion nettle stings all over her body.

Yves clasped his fingers around Cara's face and laid her on his shoulder to encourage her to suck out some of his blood.

"Come on. Come on... fuck." Yves sighed, so frustrated, realising that Cara couldn't do it.

"What is it?" asked Rose, worried.

"Cara's too weak to turn into a hunter."

"What should we do?"

"May I have your permission to brainwash her using my power?" asked Yves.

Rose shook her head; she didn't like that idea.

"If Cara doesn't suck the blood then her body will break down and kill her... but slowly and she will suffer. You wouldn't want to see that, I have seen the worst," explained Yves.

Rose looked over at Cara and hoped that she would forgive her for her decision. Yves waited with impatience for Rose to agree. Rose shut her eyes and forced herself to nod in agreement.

"Good girl." Yves turned to Cara and held his hands over Cara's eyes. A glowing light came out of his hands, bright yellow and orange, and went into Cara's eyes. Cara gasped loudly in pain, struggling to control herself but Yves was too strong for her to take over. The pupils in her eyes changed into a very light blue, almost white colour.

"Rose... would you like to do the honours?" Yves offered, keeping his hands glowing over Cara's eyes.

Rose felt terrified as she came close to Cara and put her arms around her body. With her guilt building up inside her she whimpered, "I'm so sorry, babe."

"Shut it and do it!" Yves snapped, forcing Cara's fangs out of her teeth.

Cara screamed out in pain; her newly formed fangs had caused the rest of her teeth to be so tightly pushed together that it really hurt.

He then forced her mouth against Rose's neck. Rose grunted quietly when she felt Cara's fangs break the skin.

Cara's eyes changed to a full-moon white; her mouth was forced to suck Rose's blood. Tears ran down Cara's cheeks as she did it.

Yves watched patiently; he wanted to make sure Cara sucked up more blood, filled herself up before letting go.

Cara's eyes returned to normal; she let go of Rose's neck, gasping. She didn't like it at all.

Yves was so pleased.

Rose walked backwards with her hand clasped around her neck, watching Cara.

Cara moaned as she began to feel the most unbearable pain throughout her body again. The pain was very different this time, however, not like stinging nettles, but more like being stabbed from the inside by those dangerous spikes found on desert cacti.

She stared out in confusion.

This surprised Yves.

Rose stared at her in horror as Cara's body started to tremble at a high speed and she was screaming out in agony.

"What's happening?!" Rose exclaimed.

"I don't know. Maybe… maybe her body's rejecting the blood or something," Yves replied, feeling puzzled.

"Is it because she was the first deaf vampire?"

"No, impossible. *He* was the first deaf human to become one," said Yves, pointing his finger towards a guy. Everyone turned to the guy; another vampire was standing beside him, signing what Yves had been saying. The guy then raised his hand and gave an awkward smile.

Rose frowned in surprise, she hadn't noticed that there was a translation interpreter all the time she'd been there.

Yves still had his eyes fixed onto Cara; it made him anxious to see her suffering so much. "She might just need more time to get used to it. Or possibly…" He stopped.

"Or what?" Rose feared for the worst.

Yves calmly met Rose's eyes and replied, "Or, she might die… in the natural, human way."

In the natural human way. Rose was shocked. She looked at Cara again, "No…"

Cara's body shakes were unstoppable, but they started to slow down. Suddenly she opened her mouth so wide and a scream escaped, so loud that it made the old mine tremble.

Everyone tried to grab hold of something to keep their balance whilst covering their ears at the same time; that is, everyone except the deaf vampire.

"What the hell?!" Rose exclaimed.

Cara's blue eyes changed to a milky-white colour and her fangs grew bigger for a few seconds before she quickly returned to her normal self again. She was so shocked and breathless with fear at what she had just experienced.

"Looks like she's finally got it," Yves smiled. He approached Cara and put his index finger on her cheek, "Welcome to Vampire World, babe."

Cara sobbed, she didn't know what was going on and that frightened her.

CHAPTER THIRTEEN

Later that evening, Yves left his 'room' and went to the large circular area of the old mine. When he arrived his face looked surprised and puzzled. "Who let her go?" He pointed at the empty cuffs on the rock-wall. Two vampires exchanged looks.

"I thought you did," said one of the vampires.

"No, I didn't." Yves frowned.

"What's going on?" Rose turned up and realised that Cara had disappeared.

Yves walked over the rock-wall and touched the cuffs; there was blood on his fingers.

His frowning face turned into a wide smile; he was so pleased, "Ah. She escaped by herself."

"I'm going to find her," said Rose as she walked towards the long tunnel. Suddenly Yves blocked her exit.

"Leave her be," Yves told her, "She will be back; I guarantee you."

Rose looked at the unlocked cuffs with blood dripping from them.

CHAPTER FOURTEEN

Cara walked unsteadily into the town wearing a black long-length jacket that she'd stolen from someone in the old mine. She jumped at almost anything, whenever the public transport passed her or pigeons flew past, or were noisily fighting over scraps of food, or whenever people just walked by her. Her mind felt like a water tank with goldfish inside, swaying from side to side. She had to hold on to every wall or lamppost that she passed to support herself. She looked behind several times but had no idea who she should be looking out for. She stopped when she reached an alleyway to catch her breath. Her body still felt like it was being stung all over every few seconds. She grunted and then noticed someone down the street.

She watched as two men used a hammer to smash the glass window pane of a jewellers shop and broke in. The shop alarm went off while the robbers grabbed as many jewellery items as they could in just a few seconds before quickly leaving.

The robbers stopped in an alleyway far away; they were breathing heavily. They exchanged looks, laughing. "Can't believe we actually did it!" exclaimed one of them.

"Woo!! Look at that!" The second man looked at the stolen jewellery. They laughed again, so excited.

WHOOSH!

"Wait, what was that?!" The first man panicked on hearing the sound; he looked both ways down the alley. The second man frowned; he had heard it too.

"Argh, it's just the pigeons," the second man scoffed before realising that his mate had disappeared. "Where are you?!"

Suddenly his mate's body dropped to the ground from above him. He saw blood pouring out of the dead man's neck.

"What the f -?!"

His body was whooshed up into the air.

* * * * *

Inside an abandoned building, there was grunting and screaming coming from a dark room. Cara's chin was still covered with dried human blood from when she'd killed earlier. She cried out because her body ached so much. She pounded her clenched fists on the floor and against the building walls until she was so worn out that she collapsed on the floor, breathless and sobbing.

A filthy-looking homeless man came wobbling into the same room wrapped in an old fleece blanket that had a few holes in it. He was possibly in his mid-forties but it was hard to tell because he hadn't looked after his body well. He took off his old fleece and put it over Cara.

Cara looked up at him, surprised at his kind and warm-hearted thought. "Thank you," she said.

The homeless man put his thumbs up and left the room without question, shutting the door on his way out.

Cara would, of course, prefer to be in her own house, where it would be warm and so homely. But she knew, on the other hand, that this would be the first place that they would look for her. She sighed and wrapped herself up in the blanket, feeling scared and alone.

* * * * *

Every night, Cara wandered the city streets, looking for her prey. She picked her victims carefully; they were only people who were committing crimes, trying to kill innocent people, selling drugs, or stealing stuff. She always disappeared whenever she saw vampires turn up. She still had a phobia of them - their fangs still freaked her out. She cried every morning in the dark room of the abandoned building where she slept. The homeless man would comfort her until she fell asleep throughout the day, every single day.

A whole two weeks had passed; Cara had decided that she couldn't take it anymore. She went out and found a load of free stuff in a nearby skip and brought it back to the abandoned building. She gave the homeless man what he really needed: plenty of sleeping bags, old clothes, and shoes. She wished she could do more for him but unfortunately, she didn't have any money. She wrote a note saying 'Thank you - I owe you one' in bold handwriting and left before the homeless man turned up for his bedtime. He was speechless when he saw all the stuff she'd given him and smiled, feeling so emotional.

* * * * *

A thug forced himself on top of a screaming woman down an alleyway; he was laughing. Suddenly his body was blown away from her and flew through the air before hitting the alley brick wall and crashing to the ground.

The woman was panicking; she couldn't see what had just happened because it all happened so quickly. She pulled her underwear back on and crawled backwards while her eyes searched around to see where 'it' had come from.

The thug eventually got up and pulled his jeans up quickly; his fists were out ready to defend himself. He hated it when someone interrupted 'his moment'. He looked around but no one seemed to be there except his victim who was still lying on the ground.

Then, out of the blue, Cara's face appeared in front of him; she was right up in his face.

"You -!" Thug yelled.

So that's how you treat black women? Tut-tut! thought Cara as she looked him up and down, shaking her head and tutting.

The thug almost shat himself when he heard another voice, he looked around again for this second person, shouting "Who said that?!"

Cara's fangs popped out from her teeth to horrify him. "AARRGGHH!!" He screamed.

Cara went for his neck and sucked his blood.

The woman lying on the ground looked on, wide-eyed and breathless with fear.

All the while Cara was drawing his blood, the thug's eyes had a fixed gaze and his mouth was wide open in a silent scream. She kept going until he fell down, dead. She gasped for breath; she had sucked too quickly, causing her head to feel a sharp pain as if she had brain-freeze. She wiped the blood from her mouth and looked at it, gasped loudly, and then shut her eyes in pain.

I gotta stop this, she thought, pressing her hands on her head and grunting. She couldn't stand these headaches of hers.

The woman who had been attacked by the thug stared up in horror, seeing the back of Cara and a dead body on the ground. Cara turned her head and looked at the woman who was now whimpering and crawling sideways along the ground. The woman believed that she would be her next prey.

Cara turned and saw the poor woman fearing for her life. As she approached the woman, she winced as her fangs disappeared and she wiped more blood off her lips. She reached out to her with an open hand, inviting her to take it.

The woman, still shaking, was uncertain whether or not she should trust her. She looked up at Cara who gave her a wide, heartening smile that just melted her heart so she clasped Cara's pale-skinned hand with her own. They looked into each other's eyes; for some reason, the woman felt so relaxed around this vampire.

Cara pulled off her long-length jacket and gently put it over the woman's shoulders to comfort her.

"You ok?" Cara used mime to point at the woman and then put her thumb up.

The woman realised that the vampire was very polite and also wasn't going to hurt her. She burst into tears so Cara pulled her close and gave her a comforting hug.

Suddenly Cara dropped to her knees and grunted. The woman panicked; she tried to comfort the stranger but wasn't sure how to. Cara squeezed her eyelids tightly shut, trying to hold the screaming inside.

"What's wrong? Are you hurt?" said the woman, feeling so helpless.

Cara turned her head; she suddenly put her hand over the woman's mouth and pulled her into the darkness.

The woman stared in horror; she couldn't believe that this vampire had tricked her.

Cara put her index finger on her lips to let the woman know that they needed to stay quiet and to look at where she was pointing.

The woman saw another vampire flying down from the dark sky and land just outside the alley.

"Hey, look at that!" The vampire shouted.

Cara saw Yves following and looking down at the dead body. He bent down and touched the thug's dead body. Rose turned up to see everything.

Yves smiled, "It looks like Cara did this."

The woman now knew that the vampire behind her was called Cara.

"But then, where is she?" Rose asked.

"Maybe visiting her next victim." Yves paused, "That's good - the more victims she kills, the stronger she will become."

The woman's eyes widened, she looked out of corner of her eyes but she couldn't see Cara's face.

"Let's begin the party," Yves said as they walked away from the dead body.   Cara waited, checking to make sure it was all clear before getting out of the alleyway. When she let go of the woman's mouth, the woman gave her a wary look.

Cara realised that she had given her a frightening moment back in the dark alleyway, without giving her any warning. "I'm so sorry." She spoke with an apologetic look on her face and her arms showed that she was backing away from her.

The woman suddenly felt as though she wasn't safe if she wasn't with Cara. She grabbed Cara's forearm and their eyes met.

"You, home," Cara signed clearly enough so that the woman could understand her.

The woman nodded. She was still shaken so Cara put her arm around her and encouraged her to walk in a different direction to avoid being seen by the other vampires.

CHAPTER FIFTEEN

Cara sat on the comfortable armchair with her elbows on her knees and both hands covering her face. She was trying to rid her mind of the flashbacks.

The bathroom door opened and the woman came out, wearing a dressing gown. She saw Cara sat with her head in her hands. She walked over to her, clasped Cara's hands, and took them away from her face.

Cara stood up quickly; she didn't want to overstay her welcome at the stranger's apartment.

"Are you okay?" the woman asked. Cara nodded but she was lying. "It must have been hard for you... the mirror."

It was the worst thing Cara had ever seen in her life. She had been in the bathroom earlier, washing the blood off her face and hands when she looked up, into the mirror. The reflection just showed the bathroom background behind her; she was completely invisible and it completely freaked her out.

The woman helped her get fresh and cleaned up.

"You were talking a lot when I was in the bath; I heard you," The woman explained. She was very clear to lipread so it was fairly easy for Cara to pick up what she was saying. For many years she had found it exhausting to read people's lips because she wasn't very good at it.

"What?" Cara was puzzled.

"Your voice was very clear. You definitely deserve to be with women, you do."

Cara didn't get it. *This woman heard me talking? Impossible, I haven't said anything.*

"Yeah, I kid you not. Who's Peter?"

Cara suddenly forced her eyes tightly shut because another flashback had come into her mind. The woman gently clasped Cara's cheek and the flashback disappeared.

"I'm so sorry." the woman apologised, feeling so bad for Cara.

She's so beautiful, thought Cara as she looked at the woman's dark skin. The woman giggled. *Cara! It's a bit rude not to have a proper introduction first.* Cara felt sheepish; she was just about to ask but before she could, the woman put her finger on Cara's lips.

I'm Halle, nice to meet you, Cara. It's a beautiful and short name which means 'Dear' in Latin.

Cara stared at her in shock, having noticed that Halle's lips never moved at all. *How?*

I think it comes from you. You read my mind and I heard your voice from your thoughts. So I just figured it out, that vampires possibly each have their specific powers. Halle explained this in thought.

Cara stared blankly at her for a few seconds, "Ok... erm..." She wondered if 'Halle' was okay.

I know you're looking at me like I'm crazy but I'm not, I'm serious.

"Whoa, how -" Cara realised that it was true; she could read people's thoughts and people could also hear hers.

That's right. No more lipreading, eh? Halle smiled jokingly.

She managed to make Cara smile too.

Are you okay? thought Cara while stroking Halle's forearm.

Right now I am, thanks to you.

Okay. Want me to take you to the police station or anything?

No, that's alright. You killed him so I'm good.

Cara was still freaked out that their minds were 'talking' to each other.

"Oh, I'm sorry again, do you want me to stop doing it?" Halle pointed her finger to her head.

"No... no, that's ok." Cara used her voice to speak, which Halle picked up well. "Right, I'd better go; you stay home."

"Sorry?" This time Halle had misunderstood what Cara had said.

I have to go. You stay home where it's safe for you as it's dark out.

"Oh, ok." Halle understood.

Cara trusted that Halle would stay put so she felt that it was safe for her to leave. *Oh my god, her bum... Wish I could fuck her right now.*

Cara stopped suddenly at the front door, shocked at what she had just 'heard' Halle think. She looked at her hand as it almost reached the handle of the front door.

CHAPTER SIXTEEN

Rose searched for Cara in every nightclub, pub, and bar in the Gay Village. The last pub she went into she remembered the chair that Cara was sat on two years ago; it was where Rose first met her. When she arrived, someone else was sitting in the chair.

"Oh, hello, I haven't seen you in ages," exclaimed the barman, which got Rose's attention. "Where have you been?"

"Nothing's new." Rose shrugged her shoulders, realising that she couldn't attack the people who were her own kind; she would not prey on the LGBTQIA+ community. "Hey, do you remember the lady who used to sit there, Cara? A deaf woman?" Rose asked.

"How could I forget?! You looked like you were talking straight to the wall until I mentioned that she was deaf! Hilarious!" The barman let out a small laugh and said, "Yes, I remember... such an innocent but lovely lady, that Cara."

"If you only knew," whispered Rose. She disagreed that Cara was innocent.

"Pardon?" The barman interrupted her thoughts.

She shook her head to avoid the subject and frowned. "Has she turned up here lately?"

"Hmm... No, not that I'm aware of."

"Alright, thank you anyway." Rose sighed, looking around the pub. "It's good to see that nothing's changed."

"Nah, it's not worth changing. Only fabulous homosexuals belong here and you know it." The barman smiled, "Right, off you go... Go and get her you monster!"

Rose smiled.

CHAPTER SEVENTEEN

The next night, Halle sat on the edge of her bed, staring at the massive wardrobe in front of her. She didn't know what to do and was impatiently rubbing her legs. She wasn't sure if she should open the doors yet or just leave them. She turned and looked at her digital clock on the bedside cabinet: 23:42. It was almost midnight. She sighed.

The wardrobe finally opened and Cara climbed out; she'd just woken up. She had to sleep in the wardrobe since sunrise the day before.

Halle jumped with excitement while she helped Cara to get up. Cara rubbed her eyes before looking at Halle. They were a bit awkward around each other at first but managed to smile.

Thank you for letting me stay, thought Cara, to break the ice.

"No problem, babe," Halle smiled and put her hand on Cara's cheek.

Oh, and for lending me your clothes too.

Halle and Cara were almost the same size. Cara had worn the same clothes since she got drunk and woke up as a vampire.

That's alright. I'm glad it fits you.

Yeah… Right, I think I'd better go.

Stay, Halle begged.

I can't.

Will I see you again? Where can I find you?

Don't. …Please don't try to find me.

Why's that?

Cara thought while her hands held Halle's cheeks: *Vampires will be following me and I don't want them to know about you. It happened to my ex-girlfriend, and then to me because one of vampires tried to protect me. If they find out that I'm with you, then I would never forgive myself.*

Halle looked down in sorrow. Cara put her lips against Halle's. *Thank you for last night; I enjoyed it. I mean it, thank you.*

Me too.

Halle put her arms around Cara and squeezed her back tightly, wanting more.

CHAPTER EIGHTEEN

Rose walked alone into the long tunnel of the old mine. She was smiling and still licking the blood off her lips from a recent killing of heterosexual people, whom she killed when she'd given up hunting for Cara.

Rose's face changed when she entered the big circular area. She looked uneasy because she'd heard footsteps. She turned her head and smiled with relief, "Oh, it's you… at last!" She signed before bowing, "Good morning."

Cara had appeared from the rock-wall where she'd been waiting for a short time. She smiled, first looking around and then at Rose. "Are you alone?" she signed, looking at the long tunnel.

"It looks like it." Rose bit her bottom lip; she started flirting with Cara as she walked closer to her. They slowly started to walk around in a circle, opposite each other, whilst eyeing each other up. "You look much better now."

They continued to look each other up and down.

"Where have you been?" Rose wondered; Cara didn't reply. They came closer together until Rose grabbed Cara's forearm making them stop walking.

"Congratulations on your countless victims," Rose signed to her.

Silence.

Suddenly they moved close together and kissed each other deeply.

Cara grabbed Rose's hair and pulled it back. She grunted while pushing her fangs out and bit into Rose's neck. At first, Rose moaned with pleasure thinking that Cara was about to give her a love bite, but she quickly realised that Cara was actually trying to suck all of the blood out of her.

"No!" Rose snapped. She raised her hands and used her powers to push Cara through the air and onto the ground. Cara grunted loudly with pain as if she had a stomach ache. She looked up at Rose and smirked.

Oh, now she says no, what a surprise.

Rose looked around quickly as if she was looking for a lost child but couldn't see anyone. She turned back towards Cara, "What the fuck are you doing?!" she exclaimed.

Cara got up, wiped the blood off her fingers, and licked them. Her face looked like she was still in a lot of pain.

"Say something! Sign!" Rose didn't like the sound of silence coming from Cara.

Cara just smiled. This really annoyed Rose, so she snapped her fangs out quickly.

Cara flinched when she saw the fangs. She realised that Rose was running towards her. Cara grabbed Rose's arms to try and block herself but Rose was so strong - strong enough to throw Cara backwards. She quickly got back up and they continued to attack each other. Rose's skills were better than Cara's, but that didn't stop Cara from fighting back. She tried to avoid looking at Rose's fangs.

Rose grabbed the front of Cara's jacket and threw her whole body through the air. Cara slammed against the rock-wall and fell to the ground. Rose immediately zoomed towards Cara, got on top of her and grabbed her jacket again. Cara whacked Rose across the face with a rock and rolled away from her. Rose covered the side of her face with her hand, grunting with the pain and anger. She stared at Cara in fury.

"Bitch!" Rose yelled; she zoomed towards Cara and forced her foot into Cara's face.

Cara fell to the ground again. She groaned and grunted as Rose's blood inside her began to unsettle her. She tried really hard to keep control of her mental powers so that her thoughts couldn't be heard.

Rose jumped on Cara's back and turned her body over so that they were face-to-face. Rose then grabbed Cara's wrists and held them above her head, pinning her to the floor. Cara grunted, unable to move. Rose stared into Cara's eyes, heavily breathing into her face.

Wonder what her reaction would be if she found out that Sinead killed herself two weeks ago?

Cara read Rose's thoughts and her body suddenly dropped back in shock.

Rose started kissing Cara's face but Cara was in such deep thought that she didn't fight back. Tears filled her eyes; she couldn't believe that Sinead had done that to herself.

You're all mine, bitch, thought Rose.

Cara exclaimed in disbelief when she heard Rose's thoughts.

Cara forced Rose off her, hard enough to get herself up off the ground. She tried to get away but Rose pulled her back. Suddenly Cara turned and bit Rose's neck again, making her moan.

Cara stopped sucking Rose's blood; her knees bent and she collapsed on the ground with her hands covering her face. She grunted with confusion.

Rose took Cara's hands away from her face and moved towards her lips but she got punched in the face. That made her so angry that she raised her hands and threw Cara through the air again.

Cara hit the back of her head and body against on the wall and she was stuck there by the force of Rose's power.

Rose held her power through the air as she walked closer to Cara who was screaming. She started pressing Cara's body hard against the wall. Cara lost control of her thoughts and they suddenly slipped out loud and clear enough for Rose to hear.

Fuck you.

Rose stopped and watched Cara fall to the ground.

"At last, you use your voice!" Rose scoffed before she realised that it wasn't Cara's voice. "Wait a minute... it wasn't your voice?" She felt puzzled; she looked around to make sure that she hadn't missed anyone but there were only the two of them in the area.

Rose stared at Cara, frowning, "Impossible... that innocent child's voice was you all along?! But your mouth didn't move...?"

Bravo... bravo, well spotted, Cara thought and grunted as she slowly pushed herself upwards and sat on the ground, against the wall. She exhaled and brushed the dirt off her clothes with her hand. *You fucked me for what?* She looked up at Rose, *After I told you?! You promised! And 'no' means 'no'.*

"But you're my girlfriend!"

Cara zoomed over to Rose with her anger clearly showing on her face. *NO MEANS NO! And I'm not your girlfriend anymore - you dumped me! Then you fucked me!*

Rose murmured; she couldn't find the right words to say.

Don't you remember why I hate Halloween?

Rose gulped, "Your phobia..."

Vampires... exactly. Supportive and kind girlfriends respect each other but you, unfortunately, are not one of them! Cara pointed at her old dot marks on her neck where Rose had bitten her.

Rose was still lost for words.

Oh, and by the way, my victims; I killed them, sure. But is that because I'm a new vampire? Nope. I killed them because they're bad guys. They were thieves, murderers; drug dealers. And the last one - he got himself on top of that poor woman and that was not very pleasant to watch, Cara sighed.

"But, he's still your victim; you sucked his blood!" Rose replied defensively.

Cara suddenly pinned Rose down on the ground and started snapping in her face - *I do not bite good people! Only bad people; people like you!*

Cara roared with fury.

Yves and his group were walking along the long tunnel when they exchanged looks after hearing a noise coming from deeper inside the mine.

"Quick!" Yves shouted anxiously as they ran towards the circular area.

As they entered, they saw Rose and Cara rolling about on the ground, punching each other.

"Stop them!" Yves ordered.

Four vampires rushed towards them; two of them grabbed Rose's arms and the other two grabbed Cara's. They pulled the snarling females away from each other to break up their fight.

"Bitch!" Rose shouted at Cara.

"Hey, hey, hey -" said Yves calmly as he walked in between the two angry females, trying to get them to chill out.

"SHUT UP!" Rose snapped and Cara used her loud thoughts to say the same thing at the same time.

Yves grabbed them both by the chin to really hurt them.

"I'm in charge here, you obey me!" Yves snapped.

Cara's fangs broke the skin surface of Yves' hand which made him lose his cool and he punched her in the face.

She grunted and collapsed into the arms of the two vampires who were holding onto her.

Yves' behaviour shocked everyone in the circular area; they had never seen him erupt with anger like that before.

"No one bites me until I give 'em my permission!" he yelled right into Cara's face. He then swiftly turned towards Rose and yelled into hers, "What the fuck is going on?!"

"She tried to suck my blood!" Rose snarled at Cara.

"'She tried to suck my blood(!)'" Yves sarcastically imitated Rose's speech and then continued, "You're supposed to share!"

"All of my blood, that could kill me!"

Yves lifted Rose's chin to check her skin; it was a pale greyish colour. "Indeed?"

"She sucked out all of the people's blood, but she only killed them if they were bad people. The victim that we found the other night - she killed him for raping a woman."

"Did she?" Yves looked over at Cara who was still shaking her head to try and get her senses back after he'd just punched her in the face.

"She tried to kill me because I'm her creator; I turned her into a vampire." Rose pointed this out as she'd guessed as much.

"She said that?" asked Yves while he scanned Cara's face.

"Well, no but I just figured it out," Rose said, "and also, she sent her thoughts into my head. I-I know it sounds crazy but…"

"Interesting…" Yves pulled Cara's hair back. Cara grunted through her teeth. "So, she was the one who started the fight?"

"Uh-huh", Rose confirmed.

"Then punish her." Yves turned to Rose and gave her a serious look; he still had Cara's hair inside his clenched fist.

"What?"

"Suck out all of her blood."

"All…?" asked Rose in disbelief.

"ALL!" Yves ordered Rose as he grabbed hold of her and shoved her close to Cara's face. "Suck out her blood right now!! Or I'll use my power on you!"

Rose and Cara looked at each other like it was their last time together.

I don't want to do this to my girl. Fuck, what should I do? Rose thought; she felt panicked and uncertain.

I'm not your girl anymore, Cara thought back.

Rose stared at her in shock when she realised that Cara could read her thoughts.

"NOW!!" Yves shouted in a high-pitched sound.

Rose jumped to his command and immediately bit down on Cara's neck.

Cara opened her mouth but no sound came out while Rose sucked the blood out.   Cara's hands squeezed the front of Rose's jacket. A few seconds later she could feel the inside of her body become numb and weak and her skin turned a pale greyish colour.

Rose continued to suck and as she did, her skin colour turned back to normal, a pale white tone.

Cara's eyes almost rolled back inside her head. "Stop…" She spoke very quietly, with the voice of a mouse if mice could speak. But her thoughts were loud enough for everyone in the circular area to be able to hear them.

Rose stopped sucking but her fangs were still deep inside Cara's skin.

The vampires all silently looked at Yves, who was thinking about what he should do next.

"Please… stop…" Cara sobbed.

"Rose." Yves finally spoke; he hoped that Cara had changed her mind and would apologise and join the rest of the team.

Rose let Cara's neck go and then caught her as she collapsed.

"Lift her up," Yves ordered two vampires; they did what they were told.

Cara was supported enough to be able to stand back up; she looked at Rose.

Tears were welling up in Rose's eyes and her mouth dripped with Cara's blood.

"Rose, make her talk, to see if she's changed her mind," said Yves firmly.

Changed my mind about what? Cara's mind started to speak loudly again. Everyone could hear her, even the deaf vampire. They all looked around to see where the voice was coming from.

"Well, I'll be damned…!" Yves exclaimed, surprised to hear Cara's thoughts. "About joining our team, of course."

Kiss my ass, Cara scoffed.

Yves' face showed that he didn't like Cara's attitude.

Rose… Cara stared into Rose's eyes as her thoughts said to her, *I don't want to die in front of you.*

What…?

I can't stay like this.

Please… I want you to stay with me, Rose begged.

Cara shook her head as tears filled her eyes.

Rose got close to Cara's side and begged her even more. *Please?!*

I'm sorry… I don't belong here. Please just let me go, the same way Sinead went.

"You've told her?!" Yves shouted at Rose.

I'm so sick of reading your thoughts - whatever-you-name-is, Cara thought bluntly, *Ah, Yves.*

She must have caught my thought about Sinead earlier, Rose thought to herself.

Yes but shush. Cara was straightforward with Rose before she turned to Yves and thought out loud: *'Yves'? did you say 'yes' too much, is that why they called you it?*

Yves was just about to lose his temper but managed to stop himself and turned away.

"Damn it!" Yves whispered to himself.

Rose clasped hold of Cara's pale, greyish cheeks and sent her a warning thought: *Please don't make Yves so mad.* Her thought 'voice' then softened as she continued; *You're still the same person I've known since we first met.*

No, I'm not, Cara scoffed, frowning. *We are vampires, for fuck's sake! We aren't the same as we were before.* She then sent her thought to everyone, especially Yves: *Please… please let me go. Let me go into the sunlight. That will be the last time you see me.*

Rose looked up at Yves.

Yves nodded, ordering two vampires to let Cara go. Cara fell on her knees to the ground.

Cara groaned, *Rose, please help me.*

Rose gently pulled Cara up off the ground and supported her to start walking away.

Yves clasped Rose's arm saying, "Rose, if you would rather stay with us… be careful."

Rose nodded to show that she understood. She lifted Cara's arm over her own shoulder and they slowly walked together towards the long tunnel, leaving the circular area.

It took about ten minutes for them to walk along the length of the tunnel because Rose was struggling to support Cara's weight. Eventually, they both looked up and saw the tunnel exit; it was so bright outside. Rose was so upset, she was breathless.

Cara turned towards Rose and their eyes met.

Why did you bite me in the first place? Cara thought.

"I was so angry with you: you slept with Sinead behind my back."

Who told you that? That thin, narrow beard bastard?

"Yves," Rose reminded her.

Cara rolled her eyes and scoffed, *Haha. 'Yes Man'. Rose, I've told you before... I told you when we first met, before we became vampires, that I don't like sex. Have you forgotten that part?*

Rose wanted to question her more but Cara disturbed her thoughts; she knew what Rose was about to say.

Goodbye.

Rose pulled Cara close to her, holding her so tight as their lips met; they kissed passionately until Cara stopped them.

"I love you," Rose sobbed.

I know, Cara replied in Rose's mind as she encouraged Rose to let go of her. Cara then limped by herself towards the end of the tunnel. She turned her head to give Rose a last look.

Rose was crying.

Please, Rose... Look away.

Cara watched Rose turn around. Cara turned her head and looked up at the sunlight. It took all of her courage to limp forwards, towards the end of the tunnel. She had reached the daylight. *At last,* she thought, as her skin started to burn, her mouth opened wide with the pain...

Yves and his group of vampires were standing still, waiting and listening when suddenly they heard the sound of screaming echoes and then an explosion. Yves bent his head down; he was bitterly disappointed.

A vampire signed to the deaf vampire, "Hear over there, scream echo and exploded." The deaf vampire looked down in sorrow because the only other deaf vampire was gone; now he was all alone again.

Rose fell to her knees inside the long tunnel. She cried out so loudly. "NO!! NO!!" She breathed tearfully but then her grief turned into anger. "YVES, YOU LIED TO ME!!" She zoomed back into the circular area and flew straight towards Yves, but she was too late; two vampires grabbed her and pulled her away from him.

"YOU LIED TO ME!! SHE HASN'T SLEPT WITH SINEAD, YOU BASTARD!" Rose yelled.

"So what? Get over it," Yves said as he walked away from everyone.

The group of vampires held Rose back, stopping her from getting to Yves.

"Bastard!" She sobbed, then whimpered, "If only I knew that it wasn't true; I never would've hurt Cara! It's all your fault…!"

Yves disappeared out of their sight as Rose continued to wail.

CHAPTER NINETEEN

Not far from the old mine and long tunnel, there was an empty spot that Brandon was using as a hideaway to hide in the dark. He was studying the green-coloured digital map on his laptop screen. He turned quickly when he heard footsteps approaching the hideaway. It was Sinead, carrying Cara's limp body and covering her mouth so that she didn't scream. Smoke was rising from both their bodies because they had been in the sunlight for a few seconds. Cara was struggling, trying to force herself free but she was too weak to do it. Sinead was just about to let Cara go when Cara pushed her clenched fist towards Sinead. Her fist was almost touching Sinead's face when she realised who it was.

"Thought you…" Cara signed. Sinead could tell that Cara had lost all of her energy.

"Oh my god… she's so grey!" Brandon exclaimed.

Cara fell on her bottom and was crawling backwards, crying because she was so confused.

They… Cara couldn't think straight because her mind was blocked.

"Thought the sun killed me?" Sinead helped Cara to ask the question. Cara nodded. "Yes, it would've. But I did promise you… remember?"

Cara nodded again, breathlessly. Sinead clasped Cara's cheek but Cara flinched.

"Hey, it's alright, I'm not going to hurt you," said Sinead calmly. "However, I've got someone who will help us." Sinead turned her head to make Cara look outwards.

Brandon gave an awkward wave.

I've seen him before... He interviewed me at the Police Station, Cara remembered loudly.

"Erm, yes, that's right. Brandon, my younger brother," Sinead added.

Cara suddenly had a flashback of her young bullies looking down at her, laughing.

Her mental image then zoomed in to a close-up of one of their faces; it was young Brandon.

You fuck! Cara's mind spoke out; her fangs popped out at the same time as she ran towards Brandon. Suddenly her body was pushed away from Brandon by Sinead's power. Cara collapsed on the ground; she decided to give up. She knew that her body was totally wasted; she couldn't even get herself up, let alone face another fight. She just hugged the ground and hoped for the best.

Brandon grasped his neck, protecting it as he stared first at Cara, and then Sinead. "H-h-how did you know what she said? I-I-I mean, she hasn't spoken a word yet!"

"I heard the voice from her thoughts," Sinead answered. "I believe she's possibly the first vampire on Earth to have this power."

Cara's chest was still laid on the ground, her skin was turning a worse than greyish colour. She saw Sinead approach her, bend her knees, and look down at Cara.

"Promise me that you won't try to harm or bite Brandon. We really need his help."

Help? Help, for what?

"Just trust me. Deal?" Sinead explained.

Tears ran down the side of Cara's face before she shut her eyes. She didn't know what Sinead wanted but she didn't give a shit. Her throat made an 'mmm' sound.

Sinead noticed that Cara agreed, she turned to Brandon and asked, "Are we chill?"

"I'm cool, just chillin'," Brandon replied, turning his hands, palm up, to show that he was chilled.

"Then we're even."

"Sinead… is Cara okay? I mean, her paleness is almost unbearable to look at…"

"Someone sucked almost all of her blood out."

Cara gasped quietly but didn't move her body.

"You mean… vampires suck each other's blood… *for real*?" Brandon asked.

"Uh-huh. And they kill humans as well. That explains why there are so many dead bodies around the city recently," Sinead answered, hoping that Brandon wouldn't ask too much more.

"Oh, right…" Brandon looked so confused.

Sinead lifted Cara to a sitting position which made Cara wince. All she wanted to do was to hold herself against the ground where it was most comfortable to be. Sinead removed Cara's long hair away from her face and then encouraged her to get close to Sinead's neck.

"What are you doing?!" said Brandon, panicking and puzzled.

Sinead sighed, "I'm going to give her some of my blood. Remember? Vampires share each others' blood? I'd look away if I were you."

She lifted Cara's chin onto the surface of her neck. Cara's vision was so blurred. She slowly, weakly, opened her mouth but her fangs wouldn't come out.

Brandon covered his face with his hands, but he watched in horror through the gaps in his fingers.

Cara blinked and, seeing how close she was to Sinead's neck, suddenly realised what they were up to.

Cara turned her her head away, rejecting it, "Fuck off!"

That time Brandon understood her completely; it was obvious.

Sinead turned Cara's head back around and said, "Look at me. Come on, you need some blood in you."

No, I want to die.

"No!!" Sinead panicked. Cara winced and Sinead realised that she was squeezing Cara's forearms so hard that it was hurting her. "Sorry... Look, I understand you don't want to become a vampire, I do. But... please... please don't give up."

Do you want - Cara's thought 'voice' was blunt with fury, but Sinead interrupted her.

"Do it for revenge."

Cara made a face at Sinead, a 'what the fuck?' face.

"Revenge... Revenge against the vampires who did this to you. Revenge!"

I don't want to take revenge out on Rose.

"Leigh - " Sinead sighed, reminding herself to calm down.

Cara. Cara corrected her.

"Cara, do you want them to get away with it? And just let them carry on killing more innocent humans out there? Huh?"

Cara had a sudden flashback of an innocent little boy, her nephew. *It gotta stop...*

"Yes! We've gotta stop it from happening!" Sinead said, encouraging her.

'We'? No, I can't...

"Why not?"

They're too strong and fast for me to fight.

"You just need more training, that's all. I'll teach you."

Silence came from Cara; she was so uncertain about this idea.

"Please? I can't do this all by myself."

Three of us against them?

"No, just you and me against two thousand and something."

Ok, we're fucked.

"Please, just try."

Ok... but on one condition: When it's all over, someone must kill me.

Sinead didn't like the sound of this but she nodded to show that she understood.

Promise me?

"I promise."

Cara turned to Brandon.

"Tell her you promise," Sinead said to Brandon whilst avoiding his eye contact.

"I promise," Brandon replied in confusion; he had no idea what Cara wanted.

Cara closed her eyelids, almost crying. She couldn't stand the thought of sucking another's blood, it hurt her mind and body so much. *Do it. Kill all the vampires, then I'm done.*

"That's correct," Sinead promised.

Cara opened her eyes and frowned at Sinead.

"Oh, you were talking to yourself, sorry. Take your time." Sinead patiently turned her head away.

Cara winced; she really wasn't looking forward to it. She shut her eyes, slowly breathed in and out before pushing her fangs out. Her fingers squeezed Sinead's arms as her fangs appeared because it hurt so much. She then softly bit into Sinead's neck.

Sinead grunted.

Cara opened her eyes and saw Brandon's jaw had dropped in horror. Tears came down her cheeks as she forced herself to shut her eyes and imagine that no one was watching her sucking.

Sinead was moaning.

Brandon couldn't bear to watch but his eyes were fixed on them both.

Cara's skin began to bloom from a dead-grey to a moon-white colour, the colour of a vampire's fresh skin.

She quickly stopped herself and fell back on the ground, gasping in agony.

"Fucking hell…" Brandon was shocked.

Cara rolled over wincing in pain as if she had a stomach cramp. *Why is it always like this for me every time I suck someone's blood?!*

Sorry, I don't know what that was. Sinead sent her thought to Cara's mind.

I hate vampires.

This time Sinead knew that Cara was talking to herself. Cara was crying in agony.

CHAPTER TWENTY

Brandon's big house was situated just outside Manchester, on its own, in a quiet area with no neighbours nearby. He also had a training room that Sinead was using to teach Cara martial arts moves and how to improve her powers.

For the first three days of training, Cara couldn't do anything right; Sinead was too fast and too strong for her. Sinead was highly skilled. All Cara did was fall down and get hit in the face. Every time she tried to attack Sinead, Cara missed. Her body got slammed hard against the training room walls and floor. She would also freeze or scream with fear whenever Sinead showed her fangs during training.

"Seriously?!", Sinead exclaimed with her fangs hung out, "Every time?!"

Oh, you're expecting me, now that I'm a vampire, to cure my phobia, just like that(!) Cara thought sarcastically, clicking her fingers while facing away from Sinead, refusing to look at her fangs.

"You're gotta face it somehow," Sinead sighed.

That's easy for you to say(!)

"Look at me."

Not until you put those props away.

Sinead rolled her eyes and sighed as her fangs disappeared, "They're gone."

Cara turned her head slowly to make sure that Sinead didn't prank her. *Thank you,* she thought, feeling relieved.

"...How?"

Batman is afraid of himself... Superman loses his power if he goes near... green crystal. Cara scoffed as she shrugged her shoulders.

"Kryptonite."

Wow, I can't even pronounce that word in my mind, Cara thought to herself.

Sinead suddenly performed a random attack on Cara but just as she arrived at the point of body contact, Cara had disappeared. Sinead looked around in confusion until she saw Cara in a dark corner.

Jeez! How did I get here?! Cara looked around in shock.

"This is just the beginning," Sinead pointed out, smiling.

I don't like this! Cara exclaimed in her thought voice.

As seven days passed by, Cara's behaviour became that of a moaning teenager. She really struggled to pick up whatever Sinead was trying to teach her. It had been like that since day one and Cara still had real difficulties when it came to fighting training.

Why can't I just crack their neck? Cara groaned.

"You can't crack vampires' necks - they're too strong for that!" Sinead replied.

Cara sighed, feeling so frustrated. *Why can't I just shoot them?!*

"Again, you can't shoot them - they're vampires!"

Oh, fuck this shit! Cara snapped as she walked out of the training room.

Where are you going?! Sinead sent her thought straight into Cara's mind.

I'm going to make Brandon a sandwich!

And with that, the door slammed behind her. Sinead sighed.

* * * * *

Brandon was in his study, concentrating on his computer screen. He had been working night and day for almost a whole week. He heard the study door handle turning and quickly grasped his neck with both hands to protect himself before the door opened.

Cara was standing in the middle of the doorway with a plate in one hand and the other hand holding onto the door frame. Seeing Brandon like that really annoyed her. She marched over to Brandon to terrify him and slammed the plate on his desk.

Brandon looked at the sandwich on the plate and then looked at her.

Cara moved her chest towards him so quickly that he jumped and let out a shrieking sound. She rolled her eyes before walking towards the doorway and slammed the door on her way out of Brandon's room.

Brandon let out a huge sigh of relief.

* * * * *

That same night in Manchester, Yves and his group of vampires had been attacking more victims.

Rose walked along unsteadily, she had blood all over her mouth. She was sobbing; she couldn't get over Cara's death. She was so angry for believing Yves and for destroying Cara's life by turning her into a vampire. She dropped down, putting her bottom on the step, and stared at the ground. She remembered the first night that she met Cara in one of the gay nightclubs two years ago. For years she had fucked so many women, but she suddenly stopped when she saw Cara.

Cara sat right next to the bar, alone. She was wearing a casual top and stonewashed blue jeans. Exhausted, her head was down while she was enjoying a glass of alcohol sucked through a paper straw.

"Hey, why are you so sad and alone?" Rose was trying to flirt with Cara but she didn't look up. "Tough crowd." But there was still no answer from this woman.

"I think I'd better stop you there before you continue, just to let you know that she can't hear you; she's deaf," shouted the barman through the heavy music.

"Ah, makes sense! Cheers." Rose turned to Cara, uncertain about how to get her attention; tap her on the shoulder? Nah… that would be so rude. Knock on the bar top? It would look so bad. Wave in front of her face? No, don't be stupid, Rose! Fuck, how?? she thought, panicking.

Cara was puzzled; she wondered why someone was sitting so close to her. She turned her head and saw a woman staring back at her with a look on her face like she was thinking really hard.

Rose realised that the woman had already turned her head, "Oh! Hello! You alright?"

Cara wasn't sure how to respond except to just nod her head.

"Good, good… my hands… rubbish."

Cara was puzzled, unsure if this woman meant in a sexual way or something else.

"Oh, sorry I mean, sign. You, deaf."

Cara nodded, so relieved.

"You're okay with… erm… write to each other?"

Cara shrugged to show that she was cool with it.

Rose found a table for them both to sit at and they started to communicate. Using pens and papers, they got to know each other. Rose asked her why she was in the Gay Village alone.

She found out that Cara was working at Royal Mail which she loved because of the changing daily weather whilst doing her delivery round. She also just came to the Gay Village to cool off after work before going home. Later that night, Rose suggested that she go back to her place, but Cara shook her head and wrote down: 'No, I don't think it's a good idea, but I enjoyed our conversation. Thank you.'

Rose wrote down on the piece of paper: 'Deaf can't have sex, is that right?'

Cara threw her head back and burst out laughing. She had heard that so many times throughout her lifetime. She wrote down: 'We deaf people can drive, read books, feel music, and of course, we can fuck.'

Rose's cheeks started to burn; she felt sheepish.

'However, this woman doesn't.' Cara wrote.

"What? You can't... fuck anyone?"

'Yes I can, but I don't want to. I'm not into sex. I just don't like it.'

Rose looked at her, "I like you."

"No, you don't." Cara shook her head like she knew she was going to disappoint Rose.

'Can I ask you for a date? No sex. Kissing, but no sex. That's a promise.'

Cara read Rose's handwriting and shook her head before writing down again, 'No, it's not fair on you. You love sex - I can tell. But not with me, it won't work out.'

Rose wrote something down which Cara couldn't see. Rose bent over the table so her face was close to Cara's, and held the piece of paper in front of Cara:

'Let me try, give me a chance.' Then she turned the paper round so that Cara could read it: 'I will not touch your vagina, only your lips.'

Rose gave Cara a mischievous smile. Cara looked away but couldn't help smiling. Rose lifted Cara's chin and their lips met, kissing.

"Fuck! It was all my fault!" Rose, pale white, said to herself and winced. If she had listened to Cara from the beginning then she might have just been Cara's friend rather than her girlfriend. But she couldn't help falling in love with her. Now Cara was dead, she had no one except all the boring female vampires, none of whom she found very attractive. *Only Cara.*

Then she remembered that she had lost count of how many times she ignored Cara's warnings when they got physical sexually; she tried to fuck Cara. Cara always pushed Rose's hands away from her private parts. No matter how hard Rose tried, nothing could change Cara's mind. Cara said no several times. Either that or she left in a hurry. Suddenly Rose got a flashback that Cara cried uncomfortably, when she forced her fingers inside Cara, back in the old abandon mine.

"Oh no…" Rose gasped, "I raped her."

CHAPTER TWENTY-ONE

Every night for the following week and a half, after long hours of failing at her training and the continual torture of drinking or sucking blood, Cara was in a really bad mood. One night, she entered Brandon's study and saw him cover his neck again.

Brandon faked a polite smile to hide his panic. He did that every time she stepped into his room which made her boil with anger. She approached and smashed his plate into pieces all over his desk. Brandon yelped, staring in horror at the broken pieces before looking up at her.

She lost her temper; her face came close to his with her fangs slowly coming out to terrify him.

I really enjoy making you sandwiches because I can't eat them myself! By the way, ANY vampires would bite that, Cara pointed to Brandon's neck, *That* (at his wrist), *that* (at his leg) *and that!* (at his arm). Brandon winced. *Everywhere!* Her fangs became so big before Sinead zoomed into the room and grabbed Cara, pulling her backwards. Her fangs disappeared.

I'm not going to bite him, stupid, Cara shot a thought into Sinead's mind, forcing her wrist free from Sinead's grip. She walked out of the room in a hurry, sobbing.

"Sorry, she just..." Sinead gulped, "...can't cope with the fact that she is one of them."

"No need to explain," Brandon waved in the air, breathlessly.

"We will have one hour's training, then you can go to bed, peacefully."

"Alright. ...Sinead?"

"Hmm?"

"I can hear her thoughts; they sounded like... a child voice? Innocent, but sad?"

"Yes, it was." Sinead looked out the doorway, "I think it was Leigh's inner child's voice."

"Do you mean that she was trapped in her past?" Brandon asked for clarification.

"Don't know. Excuse me." Sinead left the room.

Brandon looked back to when he was young and shut his eyes with guilt, "Oh no." he whispered.

* * * * *

Cara carelessly punched and kicked the punch bag in the training room.

Don't you start.

I said nothing. Cara read Sinead's thoughts.

Sinead watched Cara continually attack the punch bag. She came close to her and moved both of her hands, with fingers spread out and thumbs touching her chest twice, "Ready?" which made Cara stop and nod.

They moved over to the open space and looked at each other before starting to fight each other. Cara suddenly attacked, feeling outraged. Sinead blocked Cara's fists and punched her three times in the stomach. Cara grunted but fought back really hard. Her fangs grew out in her state of extreme anger until Sinead used her power to blow Cara's body, sending it twirling through the air and landing with a thud on the training mat.

"Fuck..." Cara moaned as her fangs disappeared back into her teeth which were so painful for her.

Sinead zoomed over to be her side, "Are you ok?"

Cara pushed Sinead away. She got up and walked straight towards the door. Sinead zoomed over right in front of her, Cara bumped into her. Cara punched Sinead's chest several times with frustration. Sinead stood still and raised her hands to grab Cara's arms mid-air.

Thank you, Sinead thought calmly.

That's so unfair! Cara grunted.

Over these last eighteen days, you've changed a lot. You've become so crabby, snapping at Brandon earlier and your powers have been totally hopeless. What I've taught you seems very unsuccessful. Apart from hating vampires - what's wrong with you?

I can't cope anymore with any of this! Cara whimpered.

Look, I'm truly sorry, I am.

Why me? Why is everything always about me?! I hate my life, my body, myself!

Sinead sighed, *Look, I'm sorry about the past, truly. I still have guilty feelings burning inside me, I've had them for many years, for what I've done to you.*

Why did you find me?

I didn't mean to, Leigh. I thought you were dead.

I AM dead! Cara scoffed.

I mean over twenty years ago after we found out that you were dead. I've never forgiven myself since. So... I hope you'll give me another chance.

I did forgive you, remember? In that gym changing room that they locked us in. And we fucked that night, didn't we? Our first time ever, right?

Sinead nodded in agreement.

The best?

Yeah, the best. It was the most amazing moment of my life, Sinead smiled.

Yes, it was. Cara then dropped her smile. *And then, the next night one of your friends attacked me.*

Leigh - Sinead puzzled until Cara interrupted her.

My name is Cara!

Silent.

You want me to forgive you again? Cara frowned. *Funny that. And then many years later, you found me and got me involved in the Vampires' world! When you knew that I have an enormous phobia of vampires! Still want me to forgive you?!*

Sinead relaxed her hands to unfreeze Cara's arms. Cara lay on Sinead's chest and started crying, Sinead sighed and put her arms around her to comfort her.

I swear I didn't know about my friend the night after we had sex.

I don't understand... how come you're not like that, Cara exclaimed, changing the subject.

What do you mean?

Pain! Cara looked up at her. *Look at you - you're fine!*
It... it's not so for me. That... stuff inside me, inside my head. That... it's confusing, like... it's controlling me. It makes me thirsty all the time.

"So, bite me." Sinead pulled her v-neck t-shirts away from her neck.

Cara shook her head and put Sinead's t-shirt back on her shoulder. *No... I can't stand it. It's too painful every time I do it. My body aches everywhere, every time.*

"Every time?"

Every time. And the pain... it's so unbearable just to thinking about it. Cara looked down in sorrow. Sinead pulled her against her chest again.

I'm sorry that I came into your life again, Sinead sighed thoughtfully to let Cara listen. *Also I shouldn't have left you alone that night. I didn't realised that I was followed.*

Shit happens. Cara squeezed Sinead's body and sighed. *I just don't want to stay a vampire forever. I just want to die. So those memories don't stay with me anymore.*

Sinead leant her body backwards a little, lifting Cara's neck to look at her.

It will be over soon, I promise.

Cara nodded and let go of Sinead's body. *I need to go out for a bit.*

"Where are you going?" asked Sinead.

Fresh air.

Sinead said nothing. Cara got up and walked away.

"Thank you." Cara spoke, to show Sinead that she really appreciated that.

Sinead watched as Cara walked out; she waited until she heard the front door of the house shut. She shut the training room door on her way out.

* * * * *

Cara was standing on a strong branch of the huge tree that overlooked someone's house. She saw parents watching over their newborn baby, lying in a white Moses basket.

Tears ran down Cara's cheeks as she looked through another window and saw a little boy asleep in his cosy bed, cuddling his teddy bear which was dressed as a postman. That little boy was the first thing on her mind when Sinead told her that they had gotta kill all vampires - to save humans' lives. Seeing the teddy bear's clothes made her chuckle. She sighed, got down from the tree, and walked away from the house.

Cara was walking along the park's footpath when Sinead joined her. Cara smiled, exhaustedly, *I knew you were coming.*

Read my thoughts? Sinead raised one of her eyebrows. Cara nodded. Sinead smiled. *So ...Who are they?* She asked through her thoughts but didn't receive a reply. *I saw you stood on the tree outside their house. Who's that?* But still no answer. Sinead turned around and clasped Cara's forearm to stop her walking. *I get it; you wanted to become a family.*

Cara turned away, upset, and shook her head. *No, not that.* she sighed, *That woman's my baby sister and her husband. Their baby was born last week, I believe. Their eldest son, my nephew, Rhys. Bless him... we adore each other.*

"Why didn't you say so?" Sinead exclaimed.

Cara walked away in a huff before sending her thought to Sinead's mind.

What's the point? I'm dead.

She's got a point, Sinead thought to herself before running after her.

* * * * *

Sinead and Cara went into Brandon's house after they walked all night long, chatting and catching up with each other's lives. Brandon turned up, showing them a poster.

The poster made Cara so upset.

"A report came in just before you left - her sister has reported her to 'Missing Persons'," explained Brandon. Cara walked away from them in sorrow. Sinead took the poster out of Brandon's hands.

"I'll go and check on her," Brandon said, walking away.

Sinead looked at the poster which had a photo of Cara's face on it; her face looked so happy. At the bottom of the poster, printed in bold were the words: **CARA MILES - MISSING**. There were details of her age, height, hair length, the date when she was last seen at the pub, and a contact number at the very bottom of the poster.

In the kitchen, Cara was crying, so overwhelmed with mixed emotions. Brandon approached her and hugged her. She hugged him back, squeezing him. He rubbed her back to comfort her.

Sinead was standing in the doorway, watching them, feeling so sorry for Cara.

CHAPTER TWENTY-TWO

The next night, Rose was standing on top of a very high building and looking up at the massive bright-white moon. All she was thinking about was Cara.

Cara was standing behind the training room window, staring up at the moon. She just stared at it, having no thoughts of anything. All that came into her mind was how stunning the moon was. She felt a hand clasp her shoulder; she turned and saw Sinead, smiling in sympathy.
"You ok?"
Cara nodded slightly.
"...Are you ready?"
"Not tonight." Cara started to walk away but was stopped by Sinead's hand placed on her forearm. Then Cara started to attack her; their fighting began quickly and without warning.
In his study, Brandon could hear the noise coming from the training room. He put on his headphones to ignore the noises and concentrate on his computer screen.
Sinead punched against Cara's chest to make her fall on the mat, but as soon as she touched it, she quickly jumped back up again. Sinead jumped, twirling her body around and kicking in the air, but she missed Cara who dived and rolled away. Sinead's feet landed on the mat, she ran forwards, forcing herself to jump up, pushing her feet against the wall, and flew towards Cara. Cara ran towards Sinead at the same time. They were heading

straight at each other. Cara jumped upwards and grabbed Sinead in mid-air. Their bodies swirled around until Cara pinned Sinead down on the floor with a thud. Sinead grunted. Cara grabbed a wooden stake from the back of her shorts and forced it downwards towards Sinead.

Sinead stared downwards, gasping. The wooden stake was held just above her heart without actually stabbing her. Their eyes met; they were both breathless. Sinead lay on the mat with Cara sat on top of her legs.

Cara smiled, so excited, *I… I did it!*

Sinead nodded; she was so terrified, she couldn't think what to say. Cara grinned ever more with pride as she threw the wooden stake from her side; it shot straight through the punch bag. Sinead saw it and opened her mouth in amazement. Cara looked over and, realising what she had just done, began laughing in surprise.

"Wow…!" Sinead looked at Cara, *Good shot!*

Cara's laughter faded into sorrow and she looked down. Sinead sat up and held Cara's legs, which were over her own. She lifted Cara's chin and saw tears filling her eyes.

I'm sorry, I can't…

"Face it."

I don't know how.

"Try."

Should I tell them to stop showing their thingy in their mouths?! Cara thought sarcastically.

"You're ready," Sinead signed. Cara wasn't sure if she was. Sinead clasped Cara's cheeks, "Hey," she whispered.

They stared at each other until Cara kissed Sinead's cheek.

What's that for? Sinead smiled, feeling puzzled.

I forgive you.

But I don't forgive myself.

Past is the past. Cara shrugged, feeling sad.

But now look at you; I failed to protect you. Sinead continued to blame herself. She wiped the tears from Cara's cheeks. They were silent for a few moments until Sinead heard a murmuring sound. "Your mind's buzzing," she informed Cara.

What she didn't realise was that Cara was staring at her lips. They made Cara drool and her mind went blurry; she felt overemotional and uncertain.

Sinead's fingers touched Cara's hair, just above her ear. Cara blinked, her mind suddenly stopped the murmuring.

Are you back to earth yet? Sinead smiled, testing her.

Cara suddenly forced her lips onto Sinead's. Sinead was taken by surprise by the feel of Cara's wet, cold lips. They kissed with passion and Cara lifted off Sinead's t-shirts. They carefully bit each other's lips, without their fangs coming out. Sinead then removed Cara's t-shirts and kissed Cara's pale skin. They moaned while Sinead unclipped Cara's bra and gently forced her down onto the mat. She kissed all over Cara's belly, her left, then right nipple, in her own time. She loved the sound of Cara's pleasurable moaning.

You have a big thing with your nipples. Sinead sent the thought into Cara's mind.

Fuck me.

Sinead stopped; it came out with such a surprise. "What? I thought you…"

Please… just fuck me.

Sinead bit her bottom lip; she didn't need to ask again. She kissed her gently downwards from her breasts, belly, legs until she reached Cara's clit.

Cara rolled her eyes in pleasure when Sinead reached her vagina. She had to accept the fact that she liked it. Sinead's fingers slid inside her. *Oh my God!* Cara's thought was really loud.

Sinead smiled as she continued to fuck with her fingers inside Cara and sucking her clit at the same time.

Cara's eyes rolled back in her head and then returned to the centre again; her pupils changed into moon-shapes for a few seconds before turning back to normal. She was gasping.

Please don't stop.

Sinead did what she was told.

CHAPTER TWENTY-THREE

Sinead and Cara lay naked, asleep in the guest bedroom's king-size bed. Just two hours before they had collapsed, completely exhausted from their all-night sex. From the training room to the bed, they couldn't let go of each other.

The sunlight was peeking through unclosed curtains and a sunbeam was approaching Sinead, reaching the side of her forearm. A small patch of her pale skin started to smoke. Sinead was moaning in her sleep until her mind sent a message because it was hurting so much.

Sinead started screaming before opening her eyes. She got off the bed, raising her hand toward the curtains and used her power to shut them. The room went completely dark again. She just remembered that they were so busy making love to each other through the night that they forgot all about the curtains. She patted down her forearm to put out the smoke.

"Is everything okay?!" A shout came from behind the door. It was Brandon, his voice sounded like he was exhausted from listening to two lesbians having sex all night.

"Sorry! I forgot to shut the curtains last night, but I'm fine!" Sinead shouted back, so relieved that her brother didn't burst into the room and see her completely naked.

But there was no response from the other side of the door, so Sinead took it that Brandon had walked away in a huff for waking him up so early.

Cara murmured in her sleep which grabbed Sinead's attention. She came to her side and comforted her. Cara was fighting the flashbacks in her mind. *Rose attacked and killed her by biting her... The power coming out from Yves' hand, a glowing light in front of her eyes... Four boys and a girl laughed at her... Suddenly, a close-up of one of the boy's faces - his mouth opened wide with laughter. His clothes changed into vampire-style; his fangs came out. His laughter became so scary.*

Cara woke up gasping, and sat up, with her fangs already out from her teeth. Her eyes had turned so white for a brief moment until Sinead gently forced her back on the bed again. Sinead held Cara's trembling body.

Shhh, it's alright, you just had a bad dream. Sinead sent her thoughts into Cara's mind to calm her.

The pupils in Cara's eyes returned to normal, she looked around the room then saw Sinead at her side and felt relieved that she was safe. Her trembling breath made such an upsetting sound.

Sinead was kissing Cara's forehead; their eyes met. "What's going on between you and Peter?"

Cara's fangs disappeared without her realising it.

I don't know what you're talking about.

"Yes, you do. You just called out his name a few times," Sinead pointed out, "from your head."

Cara stayed silent, trying to control her mind, to protect herself from letting any more thoughts escape. Sinead, however, managed to break through to talk to Cara's mind.

It sounds like you're afraid of him.

Cara turned over to her other side to avoid facing Sinead.

Sinead sighed. *There was also me, Brandon, Jason and Bob; all of us bullied you, not just Peter.*

Cara forced her eyes shut, she tried to block out Sinead's thoughts but somehow Sinead was still getting through to her mind. *Why did you all bully me then?* Cara asked to avoid the subject of Peter. Her face came close to Sinead's, she was really pissed off.

"Well... at first I think we just did it for fun until Brandon explained to me that Peter saw you staring at me all the time. Peter wanted us to turn against you because you were... a lezzer." As Sinead was speaking she was sending thoughts into Cara's mind at the same time. Cara flinched when Sinead mentioned Peter's name. "I didn't realise that - I hid my sexual identity because I hadn't heard of the words 'gay' or 'lesbian' until we first slept together in our school changing room. That's when I told Brandon that you were really lovely and I couldn't understand why we decided to pick on you. So, that's when we went to your house and asked you to be our friend but your mother told us you were dead."

You were not supposed to find me!

I thought you were dead! Bob, Jason, Brandon and I were all part of it, not just Peter!

Shut up! Shut up! SHUT UP! Cara bent her head downwards and pulled at the hair in front of her. Sinead could hear Cara's screaming inside her head.

Why do you only blame Peter? Sinead sighed.

Cara could feel the rage build inside her chest. If Sinead said his name one more time…

I know Peter can be a wanker but -

Suddenly Cara's eyes turned to almost all-white, covering her blue eyes. Her fangs popped out as she came even closer to Sinead's face.

SHUT IT!

Cara's mind was screaming. Her hands clasped Sinead's head which made Sinead see the flashbacks of her childhood, right up until the point when they all last attacked Leigh.

Sinead gasped.

Cara's eyes suddenly changed back to their normal blue shade. She realised that her hands were already on Sinead's head; Sinead wasn't harmed by it. She quickly let go of her head, she was breathless.

"I'm… truly sorry…" Sinead whimpered, shocked. However, she was still so confused; she couldn't figure out why Cara only blamed or was only angry towards Peter. What she had seen in Cara's flashback made her feel so sick. She also noticed that Cara's eyes had changed. *Are they like that whenever she's outraged?* she thought.

Cara, however, didn't catch that, she was too busy rocking her body. She tried to protect herself from the world.

Sinead climbed onto the bed, pulled the duvet over them, and held Cara close to comfort her.

Please, no more Peter, I don't want to talk about it - ever, Cara thought out loud, sobbing.

No more, I promise. No more, Sinead thought and promised her.

Sinead?

Yeah?

Please can you use your power to put me to sleep? And also please make sure I don't have any dreams at all.

Sure.

Sinead put her hand on Cara's eyes, a glowing light came out from the palm of her hand and in a second, Cara was sleeping like an angel. Still holding her in her arms, Sinead frowned, uncertain. *It sounds like Peter did something worse than we did*, she thought. She looked at the clock; it was still early in the morning so she went back to sleep.

CHAPTER TWENTY-FOUR

Brandon watched Sinead and Cara getting their weapons ready. As the only powers Cara had were to read thoughts, send thoughts, and sometimes be able to zoom to different places, Sinead suggested doing it the human way: to use real weapons.

Sinead approached Brandon and handed him a thick holdall bag that had wooden stakes inside. Brandon looked at her.

"Just in case," Sinead said and forced her brother to take it.

Brandon didn't want to get involved but he knew that he had no choice. He looked at Cara putting two double-end wood-stakes in the back of her t-shirt. "Is she okay?" he asked, tilting his head towards Cara.

Sinead looked over at her; she looked so sad, nothing like the cheerful 'Cara' shown on the missing person's poster. "I don't know… something about Peter really bothered her, but she wouldn't tell me what. In fact, she hasn't been thinking out loud since six yesterday morning."

Sinead anxiously looked at the time; it was now four o'clock the next morning, almost twenty-four hours since Cara last spoke or thought out loud. Sinead turned to Brandon and asked, "Um… did you send them the message?"

"Yep, they'll be there when we come back," Brandon replied.

Sinead turned her head to watch Cara. "Good... we have to be extra careful Brandon, Cara might not be the same when she's enraged. Be *prepared* for that shit."

They watched Cara touch the tip of the wooden stake, testing its sharpness; she was still looking so sad. Brandon gulped.

* * * * *

A van parked up in the empty ground of the old, abandoned mine. The van had no windows, just a front windscreen.

Brandon sat behind the steering wheel, biting his nails. Behind him was a massive blackout sheet that covered the inside of the van from top to bottom. Sinead and Cara were at the back of the van, keeping away from the sunlight. Brandon looked at his watch.

"Six a.m.," he informed them through the blackout sheet.

"They should be asleep by now," Sinead said from the other side of the sheet. She was glad that it was almost summer as the sun comes up early.

Brandon got out of the driver's seat and went into the back of the van. He and Sinead opened a door in the floor of the van. Beneath it was a man-hole cover which they then pulled open.

Cara jumped down the hole. Brandon and Sinead then began passing their weapons and equipment down to Cara below, before jumping down the hole themselves.

On the ground beneath the man-hole cover, Brandon started retching and almost threw up as it was almost impossible to breathe. "Oh my god, that smell…!" Brandon covered his nose, horrified.

"Wear this." Sinead handed him a gas mask.

Brandon put it on straight away. "Where did that smell come from?! It's not the same as last time!"

"Don't know, but somehow it's a trick, to stop humans going in to use their hideaway or to even kill the blood-eaters."

"That makes sense(!)" Brandon scoffed, as he saw Cara attaching wooden stakes to some large planks of wood. "What is she doing?"

"Stopping the vampires from getting away."

"But there's a hot sun out there," said Brandon, puzzled.

"Well, some of them can fly so fast, that they can find a dark spot to hide in until dusk. We don't want that, do we?"

Brandon shook his head; he definitely didn't want that to happen. "Will she do that by herself?"

"Not her - you."

"Me?"

"Heck, it's a really easy job. Trust me."

Sinead patted Brandon on the back so hard that it made him blink.

"What if -"

"You'll see." Sinead stopped him, her eyes telling him to relax. They set up Brandon's computer equipment and the electrical boxes so that they could communicate with Sinead through her hidden earpiece.

"Testing... testing..." Brandon was talking into the microphone.

"Receiving, Over," Sinead confirmed.

Cara was standing still, looking at one of the wooden stakes in front of her and playing with the sharp end of it with her finger.

They noticed her.

"Good luck," Brandon told Sinead.

"You too, Brandon."

Sinead walked along, sliding her hand through the hair just above Cara's ear. Cara loved the feeling, the way Sinead did that. She looked up at her.

"Ready?"

Cara nodded.

"Right. Let's go."

Brandon watched them walking away until they were out of sight. He then quickly sat at his computer, focussing on the green-coloured screen. Two dots were flashing along the screen, moving slowly through the long tunnel. He could also see thousands of white dots on the screen, in different areas. The flashing dots were Sinead and Cara so that Brandon could tell it was them, avoiding confusion.

They had almost reached the middle of the long tunnel when Sinead turned Cara around to face her. There was misery showing in Cara's sorrowful eyes.

Please, Cara... say something. Sinead leant forward, placing her forehead onto Cara's. Cara didn't respond.

Sinead sighed through her nose. *OK... look, it may be our last chance today.*

It's definitely my last, Cara finally thought aloud.

It hurt Sinead to read that thought.

By the way, you look gorgeous, Cara thought. They were so relieved to be wearing casual clothes that matched their personal tastes and not the all-black leather trousers and jackets which the vampires wear.

"You too."

Shame that it will go to waste, you know, the blood and stuff. Cara showed her the double-ended stakes.

Well, we just go in and look our best, don't we? Sinead smiled, kissing Cara's lips. Cara held her hand at the back of Sinead's head, wanting more. It lasted for a minute or two before Cara let Sinead's head go and their lips parted.

"Let's kick their ass," Sinead said. Cara agreed.

*****

The vampires were asleep, hung upside-down from the ceiling of the big circular area. Sinead and Cara entered, they looked up, and then at each other. Sinead put her index finger on her lips. Cara nodded, signing to Sinead without using her voice or thoughts, that she was going into the third tunnel. Sinead nodded. Cara walked quietly into an abandoned tunnel and along its tracks, leaving Sinead to go solo. She looked at the upside-down vampires, snarling, she was so ready to fight.

Sinead's snarling woke Yves up. He got up from his old mattress, and left the room, anxiety written all over his face.

He arrived at the tunnel and at the same time, Rose had zoomed to his side.

"What's happening?!"

"It looks like humans have found our place!" Yves looked to the other side, "Come on - to Dark Cave!" They began running through the tunnel.

At the other side of the old tracks, in the third tunnel, Cara placed a homemade time bomb upon a rock.

In the circular area, Sinead had managed to kill roughly twenty vampires. They were all laid on the ground. She was ready to fight more of them.

A vampire flew through the old tracks tunnel behind Cara. Its fangs were out as he flew towards her, snarling.

Come to me, babe! The thought was sent into Cara's mind which made her turn around fast. She threw a wooden stake through the air and then turned away to avoid seeing what she didn't want; vampire teeth. The stake went straight into the vampire's heart.

Cara gave herself a few seconds before looking at the vampire; its fangs had disappeared.

I'm not your babe, but thanks for the thought! She sent back a sarcastic thought to it. She walked along and grabbed the stake that was sticking out of the dead vampire's chest. *Don't want to waste it,* she informed the dead vampire as she pulled the stake out of its body. She put the stake in her backpack and pulled out two double-ended stakes - one for each hand, prepared for the next one coming. Suddenly, she saw more than one vampire - possible thirty-odd of them. She looked down and sighed.

Yup, I'm fucked, possibly. Come on... do it for Rhys. Just... do it! thought Cara. She exhaled and made her body disappear and then pop up again, right in the middle of vampires. They surrounded her.

The vampires were taken by surprise; Cara attacked them with her stakes.

Then more vampires came towards her and she fought them all whilst moving forwards, trying to reach the end of the tunnel. The vampires were punching and kicking while stepping backwards. Cara used the single-ended stakes to throw at them, the double-ended stakes to stab them, all the while kicking them to prevent them from biting her. She managed to avoid seeing their fangs which kept her feeling strong and her movements smooth.

One of the vampires came up from behind her, jumped, and bit down onto her shoulder. Cara grunted, then elbowed it in the face before stabbing it. She stabbed the next one, and the next immediately afterwards.

Meanwhile, in the big circular area, Sinead had stabbed the very last vampire, a female, whose eyes widened with horror as she gasped and then collapsed. Sinead was breathless, looking around at sixty-odd vampires' bodies lying on top of each other. "Where are the others?" she asked as she pressed her earpiece.

"It looks like more have gone ahead into the Dark Cave!" Brandon answered into the microphone.

"Cheers." Sinead was running towards the rocks and planted a homemade time bomb among them before going into the second tunnel to plant more time bombs.

Yves and Rose came out of the tunnel, looking out in shock. Vampires surrounded Cara as she continued to attack them using her skills.

"Cara?!" Yves looked at Rose for an explanation.

"B-b-but I saw her…" Rose murmured until Yves got close up to her face.

"Did you? Hmm?" Yves questioned, furiously. Rose looked away to avoid his eyes, "I don't think so!"

He flew towards Cara before Rose could try to stop him.

"Yves!" she snarled as she zoomed straight past him to get to Cara before he could.

Cara threw a stake at a vampire, killing it before elbowing another behind her. She saw a figure approaching her and was just about to force a stake into its chest but then stopped. The sharp point of the stake was so close to Rose's heart. Cara's eyes were twirling around and were a mixture of colours. She tried to kill Rose but realised that she couldn't.

Rose stared at her, she also realised that she didn't want to attack Cara, just to kiss her.

Yves turned up, raising his hands to blow both Rose and Cara away from their almost-kiss moment.

"Cara... My, my, my! Are you pleased to see me again?" Yves snickered.

Cara got up from the ground. *In your dreams, Mr Yes Pale Boy.*

The smirk dropped from Yves' face, his fangs popped out to freak Cara out. He loathed how Cara teased him.

Rose was staring in horror - she knew that Cara had gone too far this time.

In the tunnel, Sinead was running when she suddenly heard screaming coming from the end of the tunnel.

"Cara!" She realised who it was, zooming through the tunnel.

Yves' power, along with fifteen other vampires, used teamwork to overpower Cara. They were too strong for Cara to cope with; she couldn't fight back. They kept punching and kicking her but didn't use their fangs as Yves had instructed them not to bite her. They managed to use enough pressure to pin Cara down and then trapped her arms so that she was unable to grab them. Yves came close to her and gave her a slap. Cara grunted.

"No-one calls me a pale boy, ever!" Yves snapped.

You might need Vitamin D, so get out more in the sunshine... highly recommended!

Cara was actually just enjoying winding him up.

"Send her to Spotlight, now!" Yves shouted furiously.

"No..." Rose whimpered in horror as she watched the vampires pull Cara away from Yves.

In the Spotlight, Cara was thrown to the ground. She turned her head and watched as the metal cage door slammed shut. She got up from the ground and ran towards the vampires, but the vampires showed her their fangs. Cara froze with fear then dropped down. She watched the thick wooden outer door shut. "Fuck" she whispered breathlessly to herself. She then noticed smoke coming out of her clothes. "Oh shit."

I'm so sorry, Sinead… you're on your own, she thought but it wasn't loud enough for Sinead to hear.

"Sinead! Cara needs your help! She's stuck in… Oh forget it, I'll do it myself!" Brandon shouted into the mic and ran off, leaving his equipment behind.

Sinead pressed her earpiece, "Brandon, don't -! Shit!"

Yves saw the vampires return from the Spotlight. He turned towards Rose. "This time she'll learn her lesson," he said in his angriest tone of voice before walking away.

Rose looked out to where Spotlight was; she was so tempted to save her.

In the Spotlight, Cara stared at the sunlight. She had a flashback of some of her good memories - *young Sinead and herself in the changing rooms, having sex for the first time… Her baby sister giving birth to her first-born, in her bed with Cara's help, tears of laughter as she held the baby for a few seconds before passing it to the mother… Meeting Rose for the very first time in the Gay Village… Being a first-time house buyer.*

Those memories made her smile; she felt so heartened as she raised her arms towards the sunlight, letting it take over her body. *I am free.*

She opened up her lungs, letting the scream escape…

The sunlight suddenly disappeared into the darkness.

Cara slowly and weakly half-opened her eyes. *Oh poop.*

She saw a face wearing a gas mask pop out of the bottom door of the van. It was Brandon; he'd blocked out the sunlight. She collapsed on the ground, with her body still smoking and burned.

Brandon looked down and ran out of the double doors at the back of the van. He ran straight towards the manhole and jumped down it. At the hideaway, he sat on a rock, focussing on his computer screen to ensure that he hadn't missed anyone trying to escape out of the old mine. He put his mic to lips and said, "Sinead! I've managed to block the sunlight but I think Cara's down!"

"Great - do not do anything. Leave everything to me!" she replied.

"You're welcome(!) I'm just trying to fucking help!" Brandon murmured to himself, sarcastically.

Yves bumped into Sinead at the end of the second tunnel. He looked up and down at her; she was almost completely covered with blood.

Rose saw her and thought this was the perfect time to sneak away, whilst Yves was distracted, and ran ahead to Spotlight.

"I'm not gonna let you all get away with it!" Sinead said, walking towards Yves as he walked backwards.

"Says who?" Yves chuckled.

"Say I," she replied.

"Before we start, tell me… How did you *get away* with it?"

Sinead smirked.

She walked up the long tunnel until she faced the light. She looked down at her hand; she was holding something. When she was ready to yell, she threw the bomb down on the ground, and just as it was about to explode, she dived and escaped into another dark area.

"Magic." Sinead's answer was blunt and simple.

"Get her!" Yves ordered the vampires.

They started flying towards Sinead but were suddenly blown away by her power.

"Yves, it's between you and me." Sinead moved towards Yves.

More vampires were going after her until Yves stopped them.

"Guys." Yves looked behind them and ordered them to stay away. "Very well."

He smiled, walking towards her. They then began walking around in a circle, eyeing each other.

Yves yelled out as he attacked her.

* * * * *

At the Spotlight, Rose broke the thick wooden door padlock using a big rock, but as she opened the door, she realised that there was an inner metal caged door which was also padlocked. She looked through and saw Cara on the ground. There was smoke coming up from her body and Cara wasn't moving at all. A small fire on her clothes had started to spread.

"Cara!" Rose shouted. She raised her hands through the air which made a big lump of soil rise up from the ground and then covered Cara's body with it to stop the fire from spreading. Rose then began shaking the cage door and picked the rock which she used earlier to try and break the padlock. The padlock became loose and on her third attempt, it finally broke. She quickly opened the door and went in, her knees dropped on the ground and she looked up above. She could tell that something had blocked the sunlight. Someone had tried to save Cara's life. Rose pushed Cara's body to roll it over.

Cara didn't wake up.

"Please don't leave me again!" Rose cried out, shaking Cara's body. Suddenly Cara groaned and Rose let out a huge sigh of relief.

Cara opened her eyes and cried out, moaning because she could feel pain everywhere in her body.

"I thought you were being burned alive," Rose signed.

Cara looked down at her body then looked up at Rose, and raised her eyebrows. *I was burning 'alive'*, she thought.

Rose lifted Cara up from the ground, but as soon as she let her go, Cara collapsed again which made Rose concerned.

Give me a minute, Cara thought; she was breathless.

"Look at you... your skin...!" Rose exclaimed. Cara looked at her skin; some of it had split open and one or two bones were showing through.

Why did you do that to me?

No, Yves sent you here, not me, Rose reminded her.

No, I mean, why did you help me? Since you killed me, you've turned into an angel.

Rose was just about to say something but changed her mind. Fortunately, Cara had already read her mind.

Because you love me, Cara sighed.

Rose looked down. Cara lifted Rose's chin upward to look at her.

Rose, can I ask for a favour?

What is it?

Can I suck your blood? I'm so weak.

Rose looked at Cara's eyes and realised that she was right; her body was almost destroyed by the sunlight.

Cara came close to Rose's neck and her fangs popped out, biting through Rose's skin. Rose rolled her eyes, moaning while Cara sucked the blood out. Cara's natural eyes were beginning to swirl around slowly and change into a cloud-like grey and white colour. Her fingers slowly slid downwards and into Rose's leather trousers.

Rose was taken by surprise.

Are you going to say no? Cara thought.

I'm so sorry about that; I should have respected you.

Are you going to say no? Cara repeated the question.

I should haven't raped you.

But you did. So... want me to stop?

Rose undid her trousers using her power. Cara smiled and continued sucking while rubbing her fingers in between Rose's legs.

We gotta hurry up, Rose thought, moaning.

Leave it to me, responded Cara. She felt the wet running through her fingers so knew it was time to go inside.

Rose could feel Cara's fingers rubbing inside her at a fast pace, making her moan out loud. She didn't notice that Cara's pupils had changed or that Cara had become more enraged.

I'm coming! It's coming! Oh God! Rose's thoughts were echoing.

Suddenly Cara stopped sucking Rose's blood and fell backwards onto the ground; her body was shaking again. Her skin became smooth without any scars or bones showing.

What happened?! Rose panicked.

Cara opened her mouth and a scream escaped from her lungs, so loud that it hurt Rose's ears.

The whole ground was trembling. The vampires tried to hold their balance.

Back at the hideaway Brandon jumped off the rock seat, at the same time he let out a shriek straight into the microphone attached to his earphones, it hurt his eardrums.

Sinead and Yves fell down on the trembling ground.

"Cara!" Sinead shouted, anxiously.

"Cara's okay!" Brandon yelled into his mic to inform Sinead, as he was shaking from his hideaway.

Sinead turned quickly and blocked herself from Yves' attack.

Cara stopped screaming and bent over with aching pains shooting all over her body.

"Cara?" Rose approached her, blood coming from her own ears.

Cara realised that she could be dangerous if Rose came too close to her.

Get away from me! She pushed Rose away. She crawled towards the rock-wall and climbed up it, trying hard to control her mind and body.

Rose stood back, terrified to watch. She noticed that Cara's 'thought voice' sounded like a teenager's.

Cara's eyes returned to normal. Her arms were still holding onto the rock-wall as if she was hugging it. Her body began to calm down, but her legs became too weak to support herself. Rose grabbed Cara's waist and supported her. *Are you okay?*

I'll never get used to this -! Cara grunted. Her body suddenly jumped because she felt a sharp, shocking pain. She clenched her teeth together and winced.

Hurry, I think Sinead's in trouble and needs your help! Rose suggested.

Yes, let's go, Cara agreed, grunting.

* * * * *

Sinead and Yves were still fighting in the Dark Cave. They were both so strong that it was almost impossible for one to beat the other. Sinead turned her head and saw Rose and Cara approaching. She noticed that other vampires also saw them.

"GET OUT!!" Sinead shouted.

Rose looked behind her and saw the vampires, she suddenly pulled Cara to follow her. Cara grabbed her backpack from the ground as they went into one of the tunnels.

Yves was shocked to see Cara still alive, he yelled at the vampires, "GET THEM!"

The vampires, some running and some flying, went after the ladies, leaving Sinead and Yves to fight against each other.

In the tunnel, Cara looked behind her and saw a vampire flying close enough to catch them. Cara forced Rose down on the muddy ground and quickly ducked just before the vampire flew past overhead.

Cara grabbed Rose's jacket and suddenly, before Rose could blink, they were in the circular area.

Whoa, fuck hell...! Why didn't you do that in Spotlight? Rose thought, puzzled.

Spotlight's got a wall that I can't run through, informed Cara.

Oh. Well, thank you.

Right, if you're on my side - take this. Cara grabbed some of the wooden stakes from her backpack and gave them to Rose, and then got two out for herself. They noticed lots of dead vampires on the ground and exchanged looks. While they were waiting for the others to arrive, they were unaware that a wounded vampire was already behind them, sneaking up on them. They saw more vampires approach.

Remember what I'm afraid of? Cara sent her thought to Rose while her eye-gaze was towards the ground.

Yeah - vampires.

Yup, those thingies still freak me out. So, help me out.

Still?! But you -

The sound of snarling, screaming, and roaring came echoing through the tunnel. Rose and Cara both roared, ready to fight back. Cara lifted her double-ended stakes and suddenly stabbed the heart of the vampire who was behind them.

Jeez, where did it come from?! Cara was jumpy and then quickly focussed on the approaching vampires. She started running towards them. Rose joined in.

Brandon was in the hideaway, staring at the computer screen to keep an eye on Sinead and Cara's flashing dots, and all the other dots that were in many different places.

"There's more coming… straight towards one of you!" Brandon shouted into the mic.

In the Dark Cave, Sinead heard that through the earpiece at the same time she kicked Yves' face. Yves hit the ground, got up, and flew towards Sinead. Sinead dived to get away from him.

Cara threw a stake at one of the vampires who was approaching her. Suddenly, a vampire jumped from behind Cara and bit into her neck.

Rose quickly turned her head, opening her mouth in horror - *CARA!!*

Goodbye, Cara smiled. The vampire stopped sucking her blood, its eyes widened as it let go of her neck. Cara quickly put her hand in front of the vampire's mouth to cover its fangs. They looked at each other, the vampire was shocked, and then they looked down.

A stake was stuck inside the vampire's heart but it was still 'alive' and quickly looked up at Cara. She twisted the stake deeper into its heart, killing it. The vampire collapsed.

How rude; he hadn't said goodbye.

Rose chuckled, *Shit... never thought about how hard it would be.*

Cara nodded in agreement. Suddenly, she realised that she had lost her visions and fell to the ground, on her knees.

Oh no... Cara grunted.

Rose saw a vampire running towards them. Within seconds she grabbed him and forced his head towards Cara's face. *Suck his blood!!*

Oh, but - Cara winced. She didn't want to develop any more pain.

Come on! I can't do it all by myself!

Cara sighed, her face giving an 'Oh-do-I-have-to?' look before she rolled her eyes. Her fangs popped out and she immediately bit into the vampire's neck. Her mind became lost in a maze, her blood cells were flowing around much faster than a normal human being's would. She could see so many negative memories from her past.

Rose was watching Cara's eyes as they changed into full white eyeballs and it terrified her. Cara was so thirsty; she sucked all of the vampire's blood out.

CARA!

The 'thought voice' got Cara's attention, her bad flashbacks disappeared and her blood cells returned to normal - calm. She ended up seeing a good memory of the first night she and Rose met. They were such beautiful moments, she thought to herself.

CARA!

The pupils of Cara's eyes were back to normal again, she was suddenly shocked at what she had just done - the vampire dropped down dead just before she sucked out the last drop of its blood.

Rose looked down at the vampire's collapsed body which was like a dried-up raisin.

Cara started screaming, her hands tightly squeezing her hair. She then began pounding her fists hard on the ground.

Are you ok?

Gimme a minute. Cara was breathless as she waited for her body to 'come back to earth' before standing up.

Bad coffee?

Cara frowned at Rose but then couldn't help smiling. *Bad coffee, indeed.* She groaned as she looked outwards. Rose looked to see what Cara was staring at.

More vampires were coming out of the tunnels.

Cara exhaled, *Good luck.*

You too, responded Rose.

They ran towards them, yelling.

* * * * *

In the Dark Cave, Yves and Sinead were attacking each other until Yves forced her down on the ground.

"Aha! What are your last words?"

"I can see living people."

Yves frowned, unsure what she meant by it. While he was thinking, Sinead reached and grabbed a double-ended stake and forced it into his heart.

"Go to hell, pal," Sinead snarled.

Yves yelled as he walked backwards unsteadily and then collapsed.

Sinead got up and walked closer to the dead body. She was puzzled at herself, "'I can see living people'?! What the fuck was that?!" she scoffed.

"Sinead?!" Brandon shouted through his mic.

"What is it?" Sinead pressed her earpiece.

"Where are you? I'm not sure which dot you are on my screen!"

"Dark Cave," Sinead answered. She had given Brandon the details of the old mine with its original names so that Brandon would know and give her the directions before they started.

"It looks like Cara needs your help; there are so many vampires in the Circular area!" Brandon saw one flashing dot and so many white dots on the computer's green screen.

"Ok, on my way!" Sinead zoomed into one of the tunnels.

* * * * *

Vampires approached Rose and Cara and surrounded them both.

There's so many of them! Rose thought, panicking.

Focus! That was all Cara could think.

Sinead arrived and saw them. Cara turned towards her and their eyes met. Cara nodded her head towards the tunnel where they had both come in earlier.

Sinead looked over in that direction and then back at Cara; she looked puzzled.

Trust me. Cara sent her the thought whilst attacking a vampire with a stake.

See you at the hideaway! Sinead thought loudly.

GO!

"HEY!" Sinead shouted out to get the vampires' attention, "Come and get me you twats!"

She managed to get half of them to follow her. Sinead turned and ran ahead into the long tunnel.

Cara turned and accidentally saw some vampire fangs approaching her; she froze.

CARA!! Rose screamed.

The vampire and Cara were both gasping. Her double-ended stake had stabbed the vampire's heart and, at the same time, Cara herself was stabbed in the right shoulder. Cara stared at the vampire's fangs as they faded and disappeared. Only then was she able to relax, pushing the vampire away from her face.

She grunted, pulling the stake out of her shoulder.

Rose quickly checked on Cara and noticed that she was becoming weak again.

Cara! Get a grip!

Cara was thinking privately so that no one would hear her thoughts. *If I'm going to die, so what? I'm dead anyway.* Suddenly she saw an image in her head - her baby sister, her brother-in-law with their newborn baby. And also a nephew, Rhys. What if she failed at this war? Then they would go after her family and kill them all. That wasn't what she wanted for the future. Her body became so enraged; her lungs filled with air and forced the screaming out of her mouth. The vampires became jumpy and quickly stepped backwards. Rose looked at her in surprise.

Cara… your eyes…

Cara's pupils turned as white as a full moon again. She snapped and started continuously kicking, punching, stabbing, and throwing stakes in fury. Their fangs didn't freak her out anymore as she was almost as blind as bat.

Rose followed Cara backwards while the vampires approached them.

In the long tunnel, Sinead was killing the vampires one by one until there weren't any left. She ran upwards and arrived at the hideaway to meet her brother.

"Any updates?" Sinead asked, looking at his computer screen.

"They're all ahead along the long tunnel right now!" Brandon pointed to the dots on the green screen.

Cara was twirling her body around, stabbing one vampire, then turning and stabbing another before kicking and throwing a stake at every vampire approaching her.

Rose tried to catch up with her but Cara was too fast - all Rose could do was to stay back-to-back with Cara and attack each vampire that tried to reach Cara from behind.

Cara's emotions were building up, worse than being enraged. At first, all she was thinking was saving her family, until the bad memories of her past took over her mind, and she felt violent, uncontrollable anger. She was screaming out loudly, attacking and killing the vampires even faster than she had been before.

"Why aren't you going to help her out?" Brandon asked Sinead as they watched the CCTV in the long tunnel. They had planted a little camera along the tunnel surface earlier.

"I can't," replied Sinead.

"Why not?"

"Because she told me to protect you."

Brandon had a look on his face that said all - *Protect me from what?*.

Rose was stepping backwards, away from Cara. She was shocked at seeing Cara attacking the vampires at such a fast speed. Some vampires managed to bite Cara, but only for a short time. Whoever bit her first, got stabbed first. This continued until the last vampire ran towards her. Cara dropped both of her double-ended stakes on the ground.

Rose looked on in horror.

Cara grabbed the vampire, turned it around, and bit hard into its neck, sucking at its blood. The vampire was screaming. Cara's eyes were blurry and changing colour from white, to grey, then black.

Rose noticed that Cara's body was growing larger than her normal size.

CARA! Rose shouted in her 'thought voice' to tell Cara off.

Cara suddenly stopped what she was doing and stabbed to kill the last vampire, both of them collapsed on the ground together. The very last vampire was dead. Cara grunted, her was body trembling and she couldn't hold in her scream; it echoed around, shaking the whole mine.

Brandon's equipment suddenly blew up, smoking.

"Jeez!" he exclaimed, removing his microphone immediately, with his hands covering his ears. Sinead, also covering hers, saw everything happen.

Rose was screaming, holding her ears so tightly that they were bleeding; she was too close to Cara again.

As soon as Cara stopped screaming, she collapsed.

Rose decided that it was safe for her to run and check on Cara.

Whoa... Cara, your eyes...! You did it again.

What about them? Cara's 'thought voice' was back to normal, like an innocent child's.

They changed.

Cara winced, it felt like her brain was squeezing so tightly. Rose tried to comfort her.

Look, we did it, we killed them all, Rose smiled. Cara nodded, avoiding meeting Rose's eyes. *What should we do now?* Rose asked as she noticed Cara looking down at something.

Cara was holding a sharp piece from a wooden stake near her own heart.

Rose's eyes became so wide with panic. *Wait! Please... why couldn't we start over again?*

No way... I hate it. I hate this! Cara pointed at her own face.

Oh, come on. You're my girlfriend!

How many times?! No, not anymore, we're not. You broke up our relationship because I didn't want to have sex with you or anyone! I told you that on the first night we met.

But you've changed; you seem to enjoy sex now!

Yeah, I've changed because I'm a damn vampire and I don't want to be one!

I'm so sorry... Rose gulped. *Answer me this: W-why did you hate sex? I'm just wondering.*

Cara stared at Rose's eyes, her mind was suddenly going back to when she was a teenager. This boy, Peter who wore a vampire costume, his fangs, his black hair, and his 'devil's' laugh.

She faced the most horrible memory of her life - ever. She was feeding the horrible memory into Rose's mind.

Fucking hell... that's why, Rose exclaimed, seeing it so clearly. *But... we have a chance to change our lives, to make a fresh start.*

Cara continually shook her head because she wasn't having any of it.

Cara! I love you.

No, you don't! Cara scoffed, turning away but Rose grabbed her and pulled her backwards. Cara turned around quickly; in horror she met Rose's painful eyes.

Rose gasped. They were both in massive shock as everything had happened so fast.

They looked down at Rose's chest. The stake that Cara had been holding was stuck inside Rose's chest. Cara couldn't remember how she had the stake in her hand.

Cara's eyes and body changed back to their natural size again, tears were filling in her eyes.

"Shit, no!" her deaf voice sounded panicked as she grabbed Rose before she lost her balance, and put her down carefully.

Don't touch it... Rose grunted. Cara began sobbing; she felt so guilty. *Hey, it wasn't your fault. It... was an accident,* Rose thought, comforting Cara as they were both crying. *Babe, I want to say how truly sorry I am... I wish I'd never bitten you in the first place.*

It's too late for that, Cara shrugged - they both knew that they couldn't go back to the past.

I know... Sorry, I was so furious when Yves told me that you'd slept with Sinead behind my back.

Rose... My name used to be Leigh Smith. Sinead was my first before I... that's exactly what you saw in my flashback. I changed my name after that but... I haven't fucked anyone since, as a human.

Shit...

So..., you were the third person I fucked since I became a vampire... Cara paused, sighing, *Sorry to disappoint you.*

I slept with too many women before I met you.

Touché. Well, we're even then, thought Cara with a forced smile.

Rose winced, *Can I ask you one more question?* Cara gave her the 'go-ahead' with a nod.

If we hadn't both become vampires... the future... would we...?

No, possibly not... No, I don't think so.

Rose pulled Cara closer to her face for a final, long kiss.

Just this? And touching above the waist?

Cara nodded.

Will I see you again?

"I hope so." Cara tearfully crossed her fingers in sign language.

Rose let out a small laugh and said, "It's nice to hear you use your own voice again."

She pulled Cara's hand and put it on top of the wooden stake that was sticking out of her chest.

Let's kill ourselves and see what will happen. Rose smiled bravely.

Cara was sobbing, she forced the stake inwards to crush Rose's heart. Rose gasped before she fell to her death.

Cara began screaming out in rage.

Sinead ran back into the entrance of the long tunnel, to look out.

Cara stopped screaming and, breathless with anger, she pulled the stake out of Rose's heart and stood up. She began lifting the stake until it was a few inches away from her own heart.

"NO!!" Sinead screamed.

Cara heard Sinead's thought as her hands tightly held the stake and forced it downwards, stabbing herself as quickly as possible - the way to die.

WHOOSH! - Sinead suddenly zoomed over, pushing the stake away from Cara.

But Sinead was unaware that the sharp end of the stake was already pressed against Cara's chest, and as she pushed it sideways, it ripped Cara's chest from her left to right breasts.

Cara was screaming out from the pain before she fell to the ground.

The bloodied double-ended stake hit the ground a few feet away from Cara.

Cara looked down at her chest - a big wound. She wasn't pleased. As she got up from the ground, her fangs were showing again, but this time she was fuming.

Sinead looked up, half terrified.

Cara yelled, she ran and jumped towards Sinead but Sinead used her movement skills to defend herself.

Brandon had been peering out of the long tunnel the whole time, he couldn't bear to watch.

Sinead managed to trick Cara into thinking that she was going to punch her as she bent down, but suddenly Sinead changed her position, kicking her in the face and then continued to attack her.

Cara grunted, Sinead was moving too fast for her to be able to fight back. Cara ended up being so wobbly on her legs that she lost all control.

Sinead raised her hands and blew Cara's body through the air.

Cara's head hit the surface edge of the long tunnel and she fell down, groaning.

Sinead hoped that Cara would give up and stay down on the ground.

Cara squeezed her eyelids shut, struggling to get her head straight.

However, the flashbacks were provoked once again in her mind - *a teenage boy in a vampire costume, his face close to hers, laughing.*

Cara opened her eyes, gasped, and then snarled through her breath. She turned her head and slowly looked up.

Sinead had not seen how much angrier Cara had become and how much her body had grown suddenly.

The pupils and irises of Cara's eyes changed to an all-black colour. She got up from the ground.

"Brandon - GET DOWN!" Sinead shouted.

Cara suddenly disappeared through the air.

Brandon dived to take cover, then looked around, with his hands covering his neck to protect himself. He wasn't sure if he'd shit himself in his boxers.

Sinead zoomed to the hideaway to check on her brother and looked around for Cara.

"Where's she going?!" Brandon asked, breathlessly.

Sinead's eyes became so wide as she realised.

"Peter... She's going for Peter."

"Peter? Our Peter?" Brandon replied, puzzled.

Sinead nodded.

"We gotta save him!" Brandon exclaimed. Suddenly they heard a snarling sound coming from further down the long tunnel.

Sinead and Brandon looked out.

Yves flew in at his fastest speed, his face looked like he was very, very pissed off.

"Do it!" Sinead shouted.

Brandon grabbed a sharp knife and pushed it forwards, cutting a rope. Suddenly the planks with several wooden stakes swung down from above them.

Yves was screaming in terror. He tried to stop himself but he was moving too fast.

Brandon turned away, not wanting to watch anything except Sinead.

Yves' body crashed into the plank of stakes and killed him.

"Congratulations, you killed your very first and last vampire," Sinead smiled, patting Brandon's shoulder.

"I-I-I did?" Brandon stuttered, staring at Yves' body, "Jesus Christ!"

"Brandon!"

Brandon turned and realised that Sinead had already gone; he ran after her.

CHAPTER TWENTY-FIVE

It was only two o'clock in the afternoon but was already quite busy in one of Manchester's oldest pubs.

Two women, wearing beautiful, sexy clothes were enjoying their cocktails.

"To us!" One of them raised their cocktail glass.

"To our freedom!" the woman agreed, raising her cocktail glass, and they clinked their glasses together before drinking them.

"What do you two beautiful women have to celebrate?" A man asked, drinking his beer.

"We just finished the final assessments for our PhDs, at uni," one of them answered happily.

"Wow, congratulations! Lemme buy you drinks!"

Both women chuckled and gave him the 'go-ahead' so he ordered a round of drinks from the barman before joining them in the back corner of the pub. He sat in the middle of both women and slid his arms around each of their shoulders, checking out their breasts.

"So, tell me, what is a PhD ?" he asked, breaking the ice. The two women chuckled and he joined in with their laughter.

Cara walked into the pub with her eyes fixed on the floor. The people from one side of the pub all stared at her which got the attention of everyone else until the whole of the pub's eyes were turned on her.

The pub went silent which made the man at the back puzzled.

"What's going on?" he whispered to the two women.

"I don't know... Oh my God, that woman's bleeding!"

"And there's smoke coming from her body!"

Drip, drip, drip - the sound of blood was dripping from Cara's hands onto the pub floor. She slowly lifted her head until her eyes met the man.

The man was Peter.

"Oh gosh, she's been stabbed!" One of the customers gasped.

The pub owner, realising that the blood-soaked woman was there looking for trouble, began dialling on his phone.

"Erm... I-I-I-I see you later, yeah?" Peter said, laughing nervously.

The women looked at each other uncomfortably and left the table.

"Please hurry up!" The owner spoke into his phone.

CHAPTER TWENTY-SIX

Sinead climbed up the hole at the base of the van, to avoid the sunlight.

"Ready?" Brandon checked from behind his steering wheel.

"I am. Are you?" Sinead replied.

"Ready as I'll ever be!" Brandon raised his eyebrows, turning the ignition key to start the engine.

Sinead dropped some dynamite into the manhole and shut the door at the base of the van. "NOW!!"

Brandon hit the gas, the van's wheels suddenly spun and mud was spurting out from the ground underneath them.

Underground, the dynamite had dropped downwards, pounded onto the ground, and rolled downwards into the long tunnel. It stopped beside a tank of petrol and suddenly exploded.

The ground above suddenly started trembling. Brandon held onto the steering wheel tightly, trying to control the van as it shook and swerved all over the ground.

The explosion blasted through the long tunnel and into the big circular area, the other tunnels, and the Dark Cave. The fire from the explosion set alight every homemade time bomb that had been planted. The shaking from the underground became worse. The heavy, wooden frames and planks of wood came crashing down from the stone walls. Everything from above was suddenly collapsing.

Behind the wheel, Brandon was still trying as hard as he could to gain control. At the back of the van, Sinead kept falling, rising then falling again, and rolling about at every bump the van drove over.

Suddenly there was a loud explosion as a flame blew upward from the Spotlight. As the flame hit the air it made it even worse.

"FUCKING HELL!" Brandon almost had a heart attack but still managed to hold onto the steering wheel, but so hard that it hurt his hands. He was driving over one hundred miles per hour. Sinead was still rolling about at the back of the van; her body jumped from the floor of the van. She couldn't hold herself still.

There was a massive explosion that hurt both their ears.

Brandon looked over at the side mirror and watched the explosion behind.

"Whoa!" Brandon wowed.

"Just get us outta here!" Sinead shouted.

The ground suddenly collapsed and the old mine was completely wiped out.

The van finally arrived on the proper roadway. Brandon began laughing, so relieved. Sinead smiled but was really worrying about where Cara would be. Brandon's mobile phone started ringing, he grabbed it and threw it over to Sinead.

Sinead stayed back in the dark corner of the van, "Shut this down!"

Brandon pulled the black-out sheet, it rolled down from behind the driver's seat to put the back of the van in complete darkness.

Sinead put the mobile to her ear, "Yes? ... This is she... What?!" Sinead's hand covered the speaker, "Brandon - take us to the Grey Swan Inn in town, fast as you can! Cara's in there!"

"I'm on it!" Brandon shouted through the black-out sheet, then hit the gas and put the police sirens on.

The van was driven at high speed out of the abandoned old mine.

CHAPTER TWENTY-SEVEN

Cara stood still, and so did everyone else in the Grey Swan Inn. They were watching Cara fix her eyes on Peter, who was sitting in the back corner of the pub.

Everyone - out! Cara's 'thought voice' message was so strong that everyone could hear.

All the customers and staff ran out without hesitation. Peter was getting up from the table.

Not you, Peter!

Peter flinched at hearing Cara's deep voice and quickly sat back down. He started laughing nervously because he was so terrified. "A-are you okay? Y-you're bleed…"

Tell me… Why me?

"H-h-how you do that? W-without moving your mouth?"

Cara began walking towards him, one step at a time. Her face turned angrier which terrified Peter even more.

TELL ME WHY?! She was screaming out from her mind, showing him her teeth as her fangs came out.

"JEEZ! WHAT THE FUCK IS THAT?!" Peter panicked.

* * * * *

There were over ten police cars, a police van, two fire engines, and an ambulance parked outside the Grey Swan Inn, all with their sirens wailing. One of the police officers raised a loudspeaker and was just about to speak into it when Brandon turned up and clasped the officer's shoulder.

"There's no point using it," said Brandon. He turned around and shouted towards his van, "READY!"

WHOOSHING!

Everyone except Brandon turned around in confusion, wondering where it was coming from. Brandon, however, remained cool and calm. "Someone inside is deaf," he nodded, just clarifying as he pointed to the loudspeaker and then shook his head. The police officer just stared back blankly.

Sinead entered the pub; there was a small amount of smoke coming out of her clothes. The sunlight had caught her but luckily she ran at her fastest speed so was only burned a little bit. She could hear the sound of a man screaming like hell with pain. She could see the back of Cara, stood there, unmoved. She walked closer to her and looked over Cara's shoulder. Peter was on the floor. He knelt with his hands over his head. He was screaming.

Let it go… it's not worth it. Sinead sent her thought to Cara.

Cara didn't pick it up, however, and continued to do what she was doing.

Sinead was puzzled. She began waving her hand in front of Cara's eyes and realised what was happening. Cara was blocked from everything - thoughts, visions, and feelings. She was focused only on Peter and nothing else.

"She's a fucking vampire!" Peter gave a long, loud piercing cry.

Two armed response police entered the pub, holding guns, and pointed them at Cara's back.

Sinead raised her hand to halt them, "Wait! I got it. You'd better step back and tell everyone else not to come in until I say so."

They were surprised to see Sinead there but both quickly obeyed her orders and stepped back into the corner, almost at the pub exit. One of them was speaking into a police radio and ordered the others not to enter.

Cara's eyes widened as she stared at Peter, provoking him. She was feeding into his mind all of her suffering from the past. He was wailing loudly. Sinead noticed Cara's eyes looked so odd - it was not 'Cara' anymore.

Peter was bent down with his arms in front of his belly because he couldn't breathe. His screaming turned into shrieking.

"CARA! LET HIM GO!" Sinead shouted but Cara was too blind to see.

Peter grabbed at his own hair as he was seeing the picture of Leigh and himself as teenagers.

Peter, in his teenage years, was wearing vampire clothes, his hair covered with black paint and his face is white. There's fake blood on his lips. He smirked as he looked down at Leigh, laid on the grass.

Leigh stared at him in terror as she watched him undo his black leather trousers. "No! No! Please no!" She wailed.

"CARA!!" Sinead tried shouting again.

There was blood coming out of Cara's eyes.

Sinead could see that Cara was trapped inside a monster.

Cara's nose started to bleed but she couldn't take her eyes off Peter. Her power had become so strong that she could kill him and herself.

Sinead turned her head towards Peter, anxiously waiting for the worst to happen.

"ALRIGHT, I'LL CONFESS!" Peter shrieked.

"You better confess right now!!" Sinead shouted to drown out the sound surrounding them.

"I DID IT, OKAY?! I DRESSED UP AS A VAMPIRE AND RAPED LEIGH OVER TWENTY YEARS AGO! I FUCKING FORCED MYSELF INSIDE HER! PLEASE MAKE HER STOOOOOOOP!!" Peter bawled.

Cara's eyes finally started blinking and then returned to normal. Her fangs quickly disappeared and she collapsed on the floor.

Peter's whole body collapsed on the floor. He was breathless and wincing.

"You... how could you - you bastard?!" Sinead exclaimed. She turned towards the armed police officers, "Arrest him!"

They went for Peter, grabbed his arms, and led him out of the pub. Sinead stopped them and said, "Make sure he doesn't get away with it!" The police nodded, they understood. "You can go now - I've got her."

The police obeyed and left with Peter.

Cara laid down, coughing and gasping. Sinead knelt on the floor and comforted Cara.

"What's happened? Why did they arrest Peter for?" It was Brandon, inviting himself in.

Sinead shushed him to get him to stay quiet and look at Cara. Cara was sobbing with her eyes shut when she suddenly groaned loudly as pain shot throughout her whole body and inside her head. She opened her eyes and looked at Sinead.

"Sinead…" Cara whimpered and winced; she couldn't speak anymore. So instead she sent her thoughts to Sinead, **Kill me now!**

Cara's 'thought voice' had a desperate tone.

"I'm sorry… I can't."

Cara was gasped and crying, *You… you promised me!* It was the innocent child's 'thought voice' again.

I know but let me save you, Sinead begged.

"No…" cried Cara. Suddenly she bent over and was bawling her eyes out in pain. Her stomach felt much worse than just a cramp. To Sinead's horror, the blackness of Cara's pupils began to grow and cover the whole of her eyeballs.

"Brandon… leave now," Sinead whispered.

Brandon started to walk backwards to get away from them but to still look on.

Fangs appeared from Cara's mouth; they were much larger than before. She stood upright and at the same time, her body was becoming bigger and bigger until it was huge.

Cara... Sinead was trying to reach her with her thoughts.

I'm not Cara! My name is Leigh! Her 'thought voice' wasn't an innocent child's anymore, nor was it teenager's. It was the voice of a devil, with a deep roaring sound. She whacked Sinead so hard that she fell back and broke a pub table.

Cara ran towards her and pounded her forearm downwards but Sinead managed to block her attack by using her skills.

Brandon was anxious for Sinead's safety.

Sinead raised her hands to use her power against Cara's but soon realised that it wasn't hurting her at all. "Shit, she's too powerful!" Sinead grunted. She then tried to use the old-fashioned way to attack Cara by zooming around her, trying to trick her.

Cara groaned, screaming every time Sinead punched or kicked her. Cara tried to attack back but always missed Sinead.

Sinead punched and kicked Cara and began zooming around the pub, grabbing and throwing any object that she could at Cara until she finally noticed Cara's eyes blinking. She knew that the 'real' Cara was trapped inside a devil and was trying to escape.

It was time for Sinead to raise her hand and blow Cara through the air.

Cara hit the television screen that was attached to the wall; she fell and broke the table beneath.

"Fuck, I hope the pub owner has insurance to cover all this!" Sinead said breathlessly.

She walked along and watched the television screen fall off the wall, go straight down, and land somewhere behind the broken table. She looked over.

The tv screen was on top of Cara. Suddenly Cara yanked it, got up, and to the horror of Sinead, threw it straight at her. The tv hit Sinead and she collapsed.

Cara grunted through her breath as her body grew even larger; she was now massive.

She had become so full of rage; she was completely taken over by the devil's anger.

She shut her eyes to focus on smelling the air. She could tell that there were so many humans outside, but there was one person very nearby her.

I smell... fresh human blood. Cara's booming 'thought voice' could be heard out loud.

Brandon realised that he wished he had listened to Sinead earlier. He walked backwards, absolutely terrified.

Cara's head turned towards Brandon and her eyes opened quickly to stare at her target.

Oh Brandon, Brandon... Come on, I'm thirsty for you.

"Remember who you are!" Brandon begged her. He

knew he was unable to escape because Cara could run as fast as a plane at its highest speed.

Cara began walking towards Brandon; she was licking her lips, couldn't wait to taste his blood.

Sinead grunted and woke up; she looked up from the floor.

Cara was laughing. She snarled like a devil and suddenly flew towards Brandon.

Brandon was screaming.

Cara's fangs were reaching for his neck, and almost bit him but Sinead pushed Brandon away from her. She twirled around to Cara's back and bit hard down into the side of her neck.

Sinead began sucking the blood out of Cara as fast as she could.

Get off me! Cara snarled, struggling to get Sinead off her back but Sinead held on tight.

She continued sucking the blood while Cara was thrashing about, damaging nearby tables, chairs, ashtrays, and glasses with her movements. Cara's body began to get smaller and smaller until it reached its natural size. The colour of her eyeballs was changing continuously.

Get off me... Cara's 'thought voice' had now changed to a teenager's and no longer a devil's. The devil's face was fading away. She was breathing heavily, moaning and sobbing.

Please don't stop... This time Cara's 'thought voice' had returned to the innocent child's voice. Her eyes had returned to their natural colour. *Yes... come on, kill me right now,* she smiled until she collapsed on the floor.

Sinead let out a loud gasp; there was blood all over her mouth.

Brandon put his hands on his neck and gulped with terror.

Sinead looked down at Cara's greyish skin tone as she lay on the floor before turning to Brandon.

"Sinead... I beg you, please... I'm your little brother, remember? PLEASE DON'T KILL ME!!" Brandon shrieked.

"Don't be stupid, Brandon," Sinead scoffed, lifting up Cara's body.

"Oh." Brandon felt so awkward and then puzzled, "So, did you kill her?"

"Brothers ask too many questions," Sinead said aloud to herself.

She turned to Brandon and said, "No, I didn't kill her." Sinead explained while walking towards the door, "I just sucked lots of blood out of her so that she'd be too weak to kill anyone. Ok? Let's go."

"Hold on!" Brandon stopped her. He looked around and grabbed some tissue paper to wipe the blood from Sinead's mouth, "You can go now."

Sinead looked at him seriously, "Block me from the sunlight, please."

Brandon nodded to show he understood and he ran out.

CHAPTER TWENTY-EIGHT

Sirens were wailing everywhere outside, surrounding the pub.

Everyone was still waiting for someone to come out of the pub.

"There he is!" One of the police officers pointed out. The armed police team had their tasers guns pointed ready.

"Hold your weapons! You can all stop - we've got her!" Brandon shouted with his hands up in the air. He ran over to his van, pulled out a UV sun protection blanket, and went back inside the pub.

Everyone exchanged looks, puzzled by his actions.

Next, they saw Brandon leading someone out of the pub with the blanket over their head, it was Sinead, carrying Cara's body. The blanket completely covered both of them.

"They're allergic to the sun," Brandon informed the others.

"Shut it!" said Sinead under the blanket, relieved that no one could see her embarrassed face.

"Right... Sorry... this way, climb over," he murmured as he got them into the van.

Sinead put Cara carefully on the floor of the van, away from the sunlight. The ambulance paramedic had turned up and stopped Brandon from shutting the van door.

"Let me have a look at her," he offered.

"There's no need," Sinead said with a smile. She could tell that the paramedic was just about to say something but she continued, "Let's leave it, okay? Thank you."

The paramedic seemed very concerned for Cara's health but Brandon slammed the door on him, hinting that he should back off.

* * * * *

Brandon was behind the wheel, checking his Google map for directions.

Sinead was in the back of the van, putting duct tape around Cara's lower legs, wrists and over her mouth, just in case she woke up and started to attack again. Sinead knew that Cara wouldn't, but, *just in case…*

She watched Cara's face in her unconscious state and she felt upset. She lay down beside her putting one arm under the back of Cara's neck and the other over her chest. She wanted to give Cara comfort.

CHAPTER TWENTY-NINE

It was still daylight, with the sun about to slowly set, when the van pulled up outside a private hospital, which was a two-hour drive from Manchester. They parked in the area marked 'Ambulance Area Only' under the roof, where they could stay away from the sun.

At the back of the van, Sinead opened the double doors wide and pulled Cara out. Brandon turned up with a stretcher; Sinead put Cara on it and carried her into the hospital.

Bob and Jason, wearing blue surgical gowns, double-checked that they had all the equipment they needed and plenty of blood bags in the large cooling box. As soon as the hospital operating theatre doors opened, they looked up and saw Sinead and Brandon arriving with the stretcher. They helped lift Cara from the stretcher to the operating table.

"Jason, Bob," Sinead said, hugging her old friends, "Long time no see."

"Yeah, don't let that happen again," Bob replied.

"Yeah, if I'm going to live, we should meet up regularly." Sinead paused, looked around, and then back at them, "Erm, thank you for agreeing to help us out."

"Anything for a friend," Bob replied.

"Sinead, I just want to ensure that you're fully aware of the huge risks involved in this?" Jason warned.

"Yes I'm aware but we're dead anyway, so just go ahead and give it a try." Sinead looked at Brandon and sighed; she knew he didn't want to lose her. She turned back to Bob and Jason asking, "Right... what will you do now?"

"First, we need to take your blood and hers," said Jason.

"May I?" Bob asked, showing her the syringe needle. Sinead removed her jacket and let Bob do his job.

"Gimme a second." Sinead turned to Cara and clasped her cheeks.

I might have broken my promise babe, but I hope what I'm doing will make it better.

Sinead sighed, watching Jason force the needle into Cara's arm.

Cara began to weakly open her eyes. She had blurred vision until gradually she could focus and saw three men and a woman looking down at her. The vision made her have a flashback of the young bullies torturing her. Poor little Leigh.

Please don't torture me... Please just let me go and die now. Cara's thoughts were sent to all four of them.

Bob and Jason looked around, expecting to see an innocent child somewhere in the operating theatre, and were surprised when there were only the four of them in the room.

"It's come from Cara's mind," explained Brandon. Bob and Jason exchanged a look.

Sinead bent over to get her face close to Cara's.

Cara, no we won't torture you. We just want to save your life.

No! Don't save my life. Kill-Me-NOW! Cara was sobbing, *Please…!*

Let us do our job, Cara.

No! Please Sinead, kill me! I beg you! Cara whimpered.

I am so sorry, Sinead smiled, squeezing Cara's forearm.

Cara gasped, believing that they were going to torture her. Again. She began crying, waiting for the terrible things to come.

"Second, I need to know how much blood you each have inside you before we can start," said Bob.

"I took out almost all of Cara's blood earlier, before she could kill anyone, so she's only got a little bit left inside her," replied Sinead.

"I really appreciate that," Bob nodded.

"What's that face for?" Sinead asked, pointing to Bob's face.

"I just got both results back -"

"That was quick." Sinead looked surprised.

"We've got special equipment," explained Bob as he pointed to the medical equipment at the end of the room. "Sinead, listen - you have zero human blood cells in your body, however, Cara still has fifty percent human blood cells left in hers. The other fifty percent are not human," Bob confirmed.

Brandon and Sinead both looked at Cara.

"Y-you mean Cara's half-vampire?" Brandon asked, puzzled.

"That's how it seems, yes," replied Jason, shrugging his shoulders.

"Impossible! I've seen her. She turned into a monster back in the pub; she was so close to attacking me!" Brandon disagreed.

"Brandon..." Sinead decided to speak her mind.

"WHAT?!" Brandon snapped; feeling jumpy.

Sinead ignored him. "Every time she sucked anyone's blood, her body would always tremble and she would cry out because it was too painful for her to handle. Does that mean that her body rejected the blood?"

"I suppose so?" Jason shrugged again.

"Ladies, sorry to say... we've gotta tie both of you down," said Bob with an apologetic look on his face.

Cara had read Bob's thoughts and cried. She was so frightened and she couldn't move her body, which was now completely numb. The duct tape wrapped around her wrists and ankles meant that there was nothing that she could do about it.

Sinead nodded, she understood and got up onto the operation table and laid down.

Jason cut the duct tape from Cara's wrists. Brandon helped to stop Cara from moving her arms while Jason put the limb restraint over her wrists. Next, Brandon removed Cara's boots while Bob cut the duct tape off her lower legs and put the limb restraint on both her ankles. Bob removed the duct tape from her mouth and put a mouthguard inside it to prevent her from biting herself. He covered her mouth with fresh duct tape to stop her from screaming out. Jason hung the blood bags up, at Cara's side, and put another needle into her arm. Cara was crying the whole time.

"Sinead?" Jason looked puzzled. Staring at Cara's damaged top he asked, "Did you have any injures either before, throughout or after you became a vampire?"

"Just round my neck. However, Cara did."

"I can tell…"

"Yeah, she got stabbed and scratched and had lots of neck-bites." Bob and Jason looked at each other. "Is that bad?" Sinead asked anxiously, looking at their wary faces.

"We'll see," Bob replied, patting Sinead's shoulder.

"Yeah, we'll see." Sinead nodded nervously.

"Sinead… to be honest with you… erm…" Bob became really emotional; he was terrified to even think about it, "I'm not sure that we can bring you both back alive."

"Yeah, I mean, we've never done this treatment on vampires before; you'll be the first ones that we experiment on," added Jason.

"Hmm, it might well hurt, I mean, be very painful," Bob sighed.

"Like millions, billions of nettle stings maybe," Jason added.

"Ok, ok, I get it. Just… give it a shot," Sinead interrupted before Bob and Jason could go on and on about the risks or warnings. "I cannot stay a vampire, and neither can she." She tilted her head towards Cara.

Bob and Jason looked at each other before turning to Sinead.

"If you're dead *dead*... see you on the other side someday," Bob gulped. Jason agreed.

Sinead didn't know what to say so just nodded instead.

Bob gave her a hug and a kiss on the forehead, and so did Jason.

"Love you," Sinead sniffed.

"Love you too," Bob smiled bravely.

"Love you twice," Jason said with his voice breaking.

"Don't be competitive!" Sinead managed to make them laugh a little.

"Hey," Brandon said, stopping Jason putting a mouthguard into Sinead's mouth.
"Do you think that's such a good idea?" he asked, hoping that his sister would change her mind.

"It's Cara's and my only chance. Look, my little brother... which would you prefer? Me, as a vampire... or a brat sister?"

"Brat sister!" Brandon gave a short laugh, knowing that she was joking.

"Hey, don't be so upset. Wait and find out the end result, then you can be either upset or joyful."

"It had better be joyful," said Brandon, showing her his crossed fingers before putting the mouthguard in her mouth. "Good luck, Sin."

Sinead nodded once and Brandon put duct tape over her mouth. She looked up at the heart monitoring machine Bob had just switched on.

Her heartbeat reading was a flatline, which they both already knew.

"Look at that." Jason pointed at Cara's heart monitoring machine; it wasn't a flatline but showed a very slow heartbeat.

Brandon got close to the heart machine; he was gobsmacked.

"That's Cara fighting her own body the whole time," said Jason. "Right, let's do it."

He pressed the syringe plunger down, forcing the liquid out of the needle and into Cara's vein.

The liquid began flowing through all of Cara's veins, spreading into the deadly cells and killing them.

Suddenly Cara's body started trembling badly and she grunted with pain. Her neck muscles were pulled tight; she wanted to scream but the duct tape and mouthguard blocked her mouth.

Sinead saw this and changed her mind but it was too late - Bob had already forced the liquid into her vein. Her body also began to tremble violently.

Both Cara and Sinead wanted to scream.

Brandon put his hands over his head; he couldn't bear to watch them suffer so much. Bob and Jason were waiting anxiously; it was written all over their faces.

Sinead closed her eyes tightly shut. It felt like the inside of her body was burning. *I wonder if this is what Cara was talking about?* She thought to herself.

Nooooooo!! Cara's thoughts were screaming out as she was imagining the world was trying to drag her down into hell.

"Ready!" Jason told Bob. They split up and put the blood bag needles inside both Sinead and Cara's arms to transfer the blood.

Cara and Sinead's bodies were trembling and banging against the surface of the operation tables, creating a loud noise.

The heart monitoring machine showed their heartbeat lines were suddenly going up and down really fast.

Cara opened her eyelids wide in pain, with tears running down both sides of her face. Her eyes then rolled backwards and she blacked out.

Bob, Jason and Brandon noticed blood coming out of Cara's white top.

Jason grabbed the surgical scissors and cut Cara's t-shirt from bottom to top, lifting it away from her chest skin. They noticed blood coming out from open wounds on Cara's belly, neck, and chest. Blood was also coming out from her shoulder where she'd been stabbed and from a deep scratch on her forearm. Bob put on clean dressings, trying to stop the bleeding.

Cara's shaking became less and less until it eventually stopped. Suddenly, the heart-machine alarm went off - *Beep! Beep!*

"She's got no pulse!" shouted Jason. He jumped on the operation table and started performing CPR compressions on Cara's chest. Bob pressed on the wound around her neck and Brandon pressed on her belly wound.

Brandon looked up at his sister's heart monitoring machine; the waves were moving very fast but slowly calmed until they reached a normal rhythm.

"Sinead's passed out for a bit but she's still got a pulse!" he confirmed.

"Great - get me the defibrillator!" Jason shouted; he was more worried about saving Cara's life at that point.

Brandon ran and grabbed the machine for them. Jason got off the operation table and grabbed the two defibrillator paddles. He placed them on Cara's chest, just below her right breast, away from her stab wound.

"CLEAR!" shouted Jason.

Brandon and Bob backed away and let Jason give Cara's body a shock. But it was still flatlined.

"Do that again!" Bob shouted.

"CLEAR!"

Cara's body jumped and thumped back heavily on the operation table.

Brandon was breathless; he was looking back at the past when they bullied Leigh. "I'm so sorry, Leigh!"

Bob looked at him while Jason continued doing CPR over Cara's heart.

"Leigh? This... Cara, is *Leigh*? as in *Leigh Smith*?" Bob said, looking puzzled.

Brandon closed his eyes and nodded.

Bob and Jason exchanged looks and fought even harder to save Cara's life. They wouldn't have this, not after what happened in the past… not this time.

CHAPTER THIRTY

Sinead woke up in the hospital bed and groaned. She looked at her hands in front of her. She tried to raise her power but it didn't work. She looked up at the heart monitoring machine and could see the lines waving up and down. She touched her chest and could feel the beating. Tears filled her eyes and she began laughing, feeling so relieved.

"Good afternoon, Sin," said Jason, smiling as he walked over to her hospital bed.

"How long was I...?"

"Just under a week. Your body managed to catch up with sleep and you're reborn - human again. Congratulations!"

"No. No. *Congratulations!*" Sinead laughed, pointing at Jason. Jason chuckled. Sinead leant her head back on the pillow, "Wow..." She suddenly remembered, "Wait, how is Cara?"

Jason bit his lip.

"Jason?"

"Her body is still fighting for its life at the moment," answered Bob, turning up at Sinead's ward.

"But, will she be okay?"

"Hard to say, mate," replied Jason, shrugging his shoulders.

"After we injected the liquid into you both, her heart stopped three times, so we had to operate to fix one of her lungs and repair all of her wounds. Then she broke out into a fever and so she's still in a coma," Bob explained.

"Where is she?"

"Intensive care, on a life-support machine to help her stay alive," answered Jason.

"Let me see her." Sinead tried bending her body to move but was forced back onto the bed.

"Not yet - give her more time to heal. And for you too." Bob clasped Sinead's shoulder. Sinead sighed; she wanted to see Cara so much.

*****

Another week had passed, Brandon turned up at Sinead's ward and saw an empty bed. He could feel his heart almost drop to the floor in fear until he heard a noise coming from the other side of the toilet/shower room door.

"Fuck, I'm bleeding!" Sinead wailed from the other room.

Brandon opened the door and saw Sinead sitting on the toilet seat, crying.

"I'm bleeding!"

"What's happened?!" Brandon asked, panicking again. He didn't know if he should feel embarrassed about seeing his sister semi-naked or be worried for her life.

"I-I don't know! I just got so excited because I haven't peed or had a shit for ages and right now I'm bleeding!"

"It's your period." A voice spoke from outside the door; it was Jason.

Sinead looked down and surprised herself, "Oh! Time of the month!" She laughed, looking at Brandon standing there, "Okay, the show's over!" she sniffed.

Brandon realised he'd been staring and with a red face, he rushed out of the room and shut the door.

Jason leant against the wall, crossing his arms and smiling as he enjoyed watching Brandon's look of complete embarrassment.

"Erm… She's on her period," said Brandon, gesturing his thumb behind him.

"Hmm," Jason nodded.

"Yes… yup," replied Brandon, awkwardly.

"Hey?" Sinead shouted from inside, "Can someone get me a tampon or pad?"

"It's your job," Brandon told Jason whilst walking out of the ward in a rush.

Jason laughed. He put his face against the door and replied, "I'll get you some. Don't go anywhere!"

"You think I'll go anywhere with this?!"

Jason let out a hearty laugh.

CHAPTER THIRTY-ONE

Sinead saw a beautiful woman sitting on a hospital bed as she walked into Cara's Intensive Care ward. The woman had a baby boy in her arms.

Sinead saw that many wires were connecting Cara to a machine to help her breathe and keep her heart pumping.

The woman turned her head and with a puzzled smile asked, "Sinead, is it you?"

How did she know my name? Sinead thought, forcing a smile back and nodding.

"I'm Lisa, Cara's little sister." Lisa held out her hand.

Sinead had a sudden flashback of Cara standing on the branch of a tree outside a big house, watching her little sister's family. "Ah, of course, Lisa - nice to meet you."

"Likewise," Lisa smiled, looking at her baby.

"Beautiful boy you have there."

"Thank you. Jeremy."

"Jeremy, lovely name."

"Sinead… Thank you."

Sinead looked puzzled, uncertain whether someone had told Lisa that Cara had become a vampire or if they'd made up a story about how Cara ended up in Intensive Care.

"Made the decision, you know, took the risks - alive or dead," Lisa reminded her.

"Oh, uh… do you know what happened?"

"Vampires?" Lisa let out a small laugh, "Yes. Um… how was Cara, you know, when she turned into a vampire?"

Sinead knew now that Lisa did know everything.

A few nights before Sinead and Cara faced the vampires, Sinead and Brandon had arranged between them that their friends Bob and Jason would try and reverse the transition into vampires and make them totally human again. Sinead was relieved, if a little surprised that it had worked, it was successful.

"Honestly?"

"Please."

"Terrible. She was so terrified of being one!"

Lisa bent her head backwards, laughing heartily, "That's so Cara! Sanguivoriphobia, that's her."

"Sang-*what*?"

"A phobia of vampires," explained Lisa.

"Oh yes, she did mention it to me once or twice," Sinead remembered that Cara was struggling with how to spell it.

"Yes. I remember when she was nineteen, on Halloween Night. She couldn't stand people, not even children, to dress up as vampires. She was so shit-scared!"

Lisa laughed but then went quiet. "However, I was so shocked to find out that she'd become one, for real!"

"Only for a month, roughly," Sinead added.

"That's broken the world record for her!"

They both laughed.

"However, she did really well in the end; we managed to kill all the vampires," Sinead added again.

"Glad to hear that."

"Lisa, I want to say that I'm sorry for what your family went through, truly," Sinead blunted out, "I mean, when Cara was... erm... Leigh."

"Not your fault, Sinead; it was Peter's."

"You knew?"

"Well, Brandon told me. This Peter, he destroyed my big sister's life. I remember Leigh was so bright, happier than she'd ever been before that night. She went missing the night before until the school staff realised that she was locked inside the changing room with you. She told me it was the best night of her life. And then... the next morning, you were both found. Later that day, on Halloween Night, my parents found her at the front door, half naked. I saw her..." Lisa sighed, looking at her baby, quietly snoring, "bleeding in between her legs - dirty all over. She could hardly speak a single word. She... She just stood there. We couldn't work out exactly what had happened to her, but we knew she'd been raped. Obviously. However, the police couldn't do anything because she couldn't talk about it." Lisa looked up at Sinead, "She just... totally froze. Refused to eat, sleep or go out. So... my parents decided to make a fake announcement, that she was dead. We all gave up our lives in Manchester, moved away, and changed our surnames. It took her about three years to talk again. But we haven't spoken about what happened that night since."

"Then you moved back twenty years later?" Sinead asked.

"Yeah. Just me and Cara moved back. Don't know why but we just did."

"Lisa… you didn't change your first name, is that right?"

"Mmm. Only Cara changed her full name."

"Fair enough. What I was meant to say… Peter will be in the prison for another thirty years, maybe longer if more women come forward."

"Bastard. He deserves to stay inside a dirty prison."

"Lisa, you know what? Cara visited your house one night, to watch your family through the windows from outside."

"While she was a vampire?"

"Half-human, half-vampire, I believe. However, yes she did. But I kept an eye on her, to make sure, you know? But, she didn't. I saw her face; she was heartbroken. She missed you all. It was a fortnight ago."

She made Lisa cry a heartfelt cry, "Thank you, Sinead."

"Forgive me," said Sinead.

"Forgive and forget. You guys actually saved her life." Lisa really appreciated that she could have a chance to see her sister again. Either alive or dying, she had to see her.

Sinead smiled.

CHAPTER THIRTY-TWO

Cara opened her eyelids and saw her vision was blurry. She felt something stuck in her mouth and frowned with confusion. As her vision began to slowly clear, she could see the ward ceiling; it reminded her of when, at an early age, she was in a hospital with a broken leg - her bullies had broken it.

Cara blinked, trying to shake off the past. She looked down and saw the tube that was stuck in her mouth. There were lots of wires over her upper body. She looked out of the windows - it was dark. She suddenly had lots of flashbacks.

Rose had bitten her... Rose forced herself inside Cara... Cara sucked the blood out of the thug's neck... she snogged Halle... fighting with Rose before getting attacked by the vampires... Cara's eyes changing...

Cara panicked, realised that she was still 'undead'.

She pulled the tube out of her mouth, coughing violently, and removed all of the wires from her body. She didn't realise but the heart machine alarm had gone off. She got off the bed and fell on the flooring, grunting. *Not this again!* she thought as all the pain from before returned. She pulled herself up and ran out of the ward.

Cara ran down the hospital hallway. In the distance, she could see the doctors and nurses running towards her ward so she quickly opened the door to an empty room and crept inside to hide from them. She waited until the corridor was clear before returning to the hallway.

Bob and Jason ran into Cara's ward. A doctor said to them, "The patient's not here!"

"Call security to lockdown right now! Her body didn't heal properly!" Bob shouted.

A doctor ran out and passed Sinead on the way out.

"What's going on?" She was puzzled.

"Cara's escaping," said Jason.

Sinead ran out of the ward.

* * * * *

On the ground floor waiting room, Cara had almost reached the hospital back doorway when she noticed a security guard standing next to the doors, which were also locked. She hid quickly behind the wall and looked up at the window; it was still dark. She had a sudden flashback of stabbing Rose to death. She squeezed her eyelids shut, trying to ignore it. Either her vision had become blurry or her head was dizzy; she couldn't tell the difference. Suddenly she bent over and threw up blood on the floor. Again, she had a flashback of herself sucking the vampire's blood. She then bent and crawled backwards away from the blood. She was gasping for breath with her hand pressed down on her chest. As she forced herself up, she sneaked a glance at the security guard in the distance. He turned away, so she sneaked into the cafe's kitchen as quickly as she could.

In the kitchen, Cara ran and slid under the metal table. Her left shoulder had become so tight that it made her arm numb. Still struggling for air, Cara was gasping heavily and vomited blood again. Crying, she looked around for something and saw a big knife on a wall against a magnet. She forced herself upward and grabbed the knife. She turned it around and pointed the sharp end against her chest. Suddenly she looked ahead and saw her reflection on a metal surface. She was puzzled, shocked to see herself. Her vision had begun to fade, she blinked and, before she knew it, she was on the floor.

Opening her eyes, Cara noticed someone's shoes stepping into the kitchen. She shut her eyes.

Opening her eyes again, she saw Sinead's face looking down at her as the ceiling above circled around several times. Cara shut her eyes again.

Opening her eyes again, she saw the operating room with people surrounding her. *Not again,* she thought before shutting her eyes.

CHAPTER THIRTY-THREE

The next morning, Cara opened her eyes weakly and found herself in a different ward and with an oxygen mask on her face. She looked down and saw limb restraints on her ankles. This puzzled her; she wondered what they were there for. But then she remembered that she'd tried to escape and it was to make sure that she wouldn't do that again. She was puzzled - *How long ago was it?* She couldn't be thinking straight. *Was I drugged?* She tried to remove the oxygen mask but was too weak to do so. She looked up at the heart monitoring machine. *I have a heartbeat? Impossible.* She moaned, closed her eyes, and hoped to die.

Suddenly the ward's light was switched on. Cara squeezed her eyelids together for a few seconds before opening them a bit to try and see what was going on. A small hand popped out of the ward doorway holding some envelopes.

Cara was puzzled and frightened until the face of a six-year-old boy popped out of the doorway. Cara suddenly became so emotional to see her nephew Rhys again. He marched into her ward wearing his postman's uniform; Cara loved seeing him dress up as a postman. He raised up his arm, his hands full of envelopes, approaching Cara. He laid the envelopes on the bed, freeing his hands to sign.

"You have ten letters today," said Rhys.

Cara let out a small laugh and managed to show him her hand with a thumb up and then changed to a pinky finger.

"Good or bad?" he asked, making sure. Cara nodded lightly. He looked at the envelopes on the bed and scratched his head. "Good letters, maybe?"

Cara laughed, feeling heartened, and then winced forgetting she was still in pain.

"Are you okay? Did I make you laugh too much?"

Cara laughed quietly, forcing her hards to start signing, "Always."

His grinning face melted her heart. He climbed up and, realising he wanted a hug, Cara freaked out.

"Wait!" Cara spoke with her deaf voice.

The innocent eyes of this beautiful boy looked right into Cara's. He was so confused and possibly a bit upset.

Sinead showed up in the ward and saw what was happening.

"No, that's ok, Rhys, go on, but hug gently; your auntie isn't so well." Sinead signed for Cara and spoke for Rhys.

Rhys looked at Cara to give permission; she could tell. She missed him so much and needed a hug. She gave him a nod. He climbed on the bed and got to her for a cuddle. Cara was still freaked out. She clenched her jaw together tightly, trying to control herself and her fast heart rate. She looked at Sinead, frozen stiff with fear.   "H e y. I can't hear your thoughts anymore, and neither can you." Sinead signed without using her voice because she didn't want Rhys to hear their conversation.

Care was puzzled, confused.

"See the light, we don't burn anymore," Sinead smiled, "You and me - we're back to being human again."

Tears filled Cara's eyes, she was unsure if this was real or just a dream. "Are you sure?"

Sinead nodded. Cara gasped with joy and looked down at Rhys' head resting against her right shoulder. She clasped his head and he looked up at her. His innocent beautiful face. She pulled him up for a proper hug, and squeezing him tightly, she realised she'd forgotten all about the pain she was in. She wailed.

"I'm sorry!" Rhys said panicked and moving away from Cara.

"No, it's not you, it's just that Cara's body is still so sore," said Sinead, comforting Rhys.

Cara anxiously put her hand on her chest.

"What happened to me?" she asked Sinead in confusion.

"You had an operation last night and one of your lungs collapsed again," Sinead replied, "but Bob and Jason did another brilliant job... As long as you're not planning to run off again!" she added, teasing Cara.

"I thought -"

"That you're still a vampire? I know, but not anymore."

"Thought you fixed me?"

Sinead sighed and explained, "When our bodies switch back to being human again, all the powers we had as vampires disappear. So our bodies go back to normal, which means, for you, well, all the wounds you had previously come back again. You were almost dead *dead* on the operating table."

Cara looked down but her head was blank; she couldn't think of anything.

She then looked at Rhys and realised she'd had him so upset.

"I'm sorry," she said and opened her arm wide to let Rhys come and give his auntie a huge hug.

Sinead smiled.

CHAPTER THIRTY-FOUR

A summer chair. Suncream. A lesbian novel. A glass of water and ice cream. And, of course, hot sunshine. That's exactly what Cara wanted, a blissful day chilling out in her little sister's back garden. She watched her nephew Rhys playing with his toys in the sandbox. She smiled but sadly. To lose Rose was so painful to think about. She didn't know what to say to Rose's family about Rose's body. Sinead and Brandon couldn't tell the family the whole truth, so the family went ahead with Rose's funeral, saying farewell to an empty coffin.

Cara was also thinking about something else - her scars. She was wearing a vest and shorts; there were lots of scars showing on her neck, chest, shoulders, and her forearm. Her scars bothered her a lot. She didn't mind showing her bare skin in Lisa's gardens but never out in public or in front of other people. However, it wasn't only that which was bothering her - what really bothered her was that something was missing. With tears rolling down her cheeks, she leant back and let the sunshine take over her body.

* * * * *

Cara sat, surrounded by her family, at dinner time. Cara was staring, being so quiet until Lisa got her attention.

"Are you okay?" her sister asked.

"Sorry, was miles away," replied Cara, realising that she was eating much more slowly than the rest of her family.

"What's wrong?"

"I'm just not hungry, I think."

"No, I mean, what's wrong?" Lisa asked Cara again, giving her an encouraging smile.

The table was silent.

Cara sighed, "I'm ready."

"Ready for what?"

"To go back to my house, back to work," answered Cara.

Lisa smiled.

"Don't be offended. I've loved spending my time here, loved hanging out with you all. I love all of you too. But... I need to go back to where I belong - in my own home, my job, back to my everyday life. It's been two months, so I'm ready."

"Hey, all I want is to see you happy. I'm here if you need anything." Lisa smiled, squeezing her big sister's hand.

Cara smiled, feeling glad, "Thank you."

CHAPTER THIRTY-FIVE

Cara arrived outside her own house; she was so pleased to be back there again. She walked along her footpath and stopped. Looking down at her footpath, Cara had a flashback of Sinead, terrifying her, she believed that Sinead would hurt her again, even though years had passed.

Reaching the front door, she shut her eyes and exhaled through her nose. She unlocked the door using the spare set of keys that her sister kept in an emergency. That was lucky, she thought, because she left the house without her keys when she'd turned into a vampire. She opened the door and looked down at the floor. She had a flashback of when Cara forced Sinead down on the floor to save her from the sunlight.

She remembered seeing Sinead's face, skin and flesh burned off by the sunlight, and her skull showing through.

Cara gulped and wondered what, in her visual memories, she was going to 'see' from the past next. The living room - she could 'see' Sinead comfort her after Cara found out that Rose was murdered which puzzled her, on this point her memories were very blurry.

The kitchen - she could 'see' Sinead's fangs disappearing after the knife stabbed in Cara's belly.

Tears filled Cara's eyes as she shut her front door and locked it before going up the stairs.

When she arrived at the top of the stairs she looked at the bathroom. Sinead stood there long enough to give her a heart attack. She wondered why she didn't see Sinead's reflection in the mirror, but then remembered that Sinead was a vampire.

Cara turned into her bedroom and could see Sinead everywhere - a chair, their first kiss, being half-naked together.

Cara lay on her bed. *So glad to be in my own bed tonight!* she thought. She turned around to other side and looked at the pillow. She 'saw' Sinead lying right there. On her own bed.

Closing her eyes, Cara let the flashback to take over her mind. She was gently breathless and licked her lips.

"No sex?" Sinead was puzzled. Cara nodded, staring at Sinead's chest; she was wearing just a bra. Cara then looked at Sinead's soft cold-blue lips. She could feel that her boxer shorts had become so wet. There was so much buzzing around in her mind. She wanted to kiss Sinead so badly, she pulled the back of Sinead's neck towards her to kiss her lips. Sinead's hands went behind Cara's back, pulling her in so tightly, breasts to breasts. Their bodies rubbing together made Cara lose her patience; she pulled her own t-shirt away. Sinead kissed upon Cara's shoulder which tickled her and she moaned. She undid Sinead's bra and seeing her beautiful breasts made Cara's lips so wet, she ignored the troubling feeling down below. She licked around the nipple before sucking them. Sinead bent her head backwards and moaned, which Cara saw. She unclipped her own bra and Sinead noticed. Sinead clasped

Cara's breasts whilst Cara sucked hers. Sinead squeezing and rubbing all around Cara's nipple. Cara's mouth was then freed from Sinead's nipple which gave Sinead a turn at kissing around Cara's breasts.

Cara loved it - she loved this feeling. Moaning, she could felt Sinead's teeth bite gently into her nipple. "Oh, god!" Cara gasped. She knew Sinead had heard it because she felt the sound vibration through her own throat.

They climbed onto the bed, Sinead got on top of her. Cara started to feel wary but, at the same time, didn't want to spoil the enjoyment she was feeling just having the physical connection with her. Sinead kissed Cara's lips, then down her neck, shoulder, breast, and belly. Cara's nervous and unsettling feelings were now building up, so she shut her eyes to try to get them under control. She didn't want to push Sinead away like she did Rose.

Sinead kissed over Cara's boxers, just above the public hair. It tickled Cara so much but she was also worried that Sinead might go too far, but, she didn't. She kissed upon Cara's leg. Cara then became so relaxed and was enjoying Sinead's kissing her all over her naked body, everywhere except in her boxers.

Finally, Sinead returned to Cara's face and their eyes met, breathlessly.

Cara's fingers were rubbing rhythmically inside her boxers; she was alone in bed. She was moaning, wanting Sinead - so badly.

CHAPTER THIRTY-SIX

In an abandoned building, a homeless man was lying on a mattress with a couple of sleeping bags. He was woken up by a few strangers.

"Leave me alone!" he shouted, panicking. He was afraid of having to sleep on the streets again or even worse - being abused by the strangers.

"Hey, Sir. We're here to help you."

"...What?" He stared at them.

"Are you Terry?" one of them asked.

"... Yes, it's me."

"Terry, I would like you to follow us; there's something we want to show you."

"But, my things..."

"Don't worry about that, trust us."

They took him to a bedsit flat which was about twenty-minute drive from the abandoned building. He walked in and looked around in confusion, mumbling under his breath. One of the strangers gave him the keys. He stared at the keys and then looked up, frowning uncertainly, not wanting to get his hopes up.

"It's your flat," said the assistant.

"But... I can't afford, erm, the rent or anything," he replied.

"Don't you worry about that just now. Your new clothes are in the shower room. Meet us downstairs and we will take you somewhere."

Terry looked around, too emotional to take it all in. "What time should I meet you downstairs?"

"It's 8 am, let's say in three hours? Or four?"

"Noon will be fine with me," Terry said, wanting to get it over with.

"Sure. Your breakfast is over there."

He looked over and saw the table that had been prepared for him. "Yes, I guess I'll go for a shower first."

"Help yourself - this flat's all yours," the assistant smiled, "See you downstairs."

Terry watched them walk out and shut the door behind them.

He looked around at his bedsit, laughing with so much happiness.

In the early afternoon, Terry, the former homeless man, who now looked so young without a beard, with the help of his assistants had his hair cut at a professional barber's. He arrived in the building wearing his fresh clothes. He couldn't believe how quickly he could go from being homeless and broke to having his own bedsit and fresh new look.

Now he was on his way to meet more strangers, he was nervous but received so much support from the assistants.

"Hello there, stranger!" Cara's boss said, approaching Terry and reaching out his hand to shake his. "Cara's told me a lot about you. All good, just to let you know!" he added, smiling.

"Cara?" Terry wondered if it was the same person or not.

"Yes, Cara, she suggested that I offer you a job if you're happy to take that opportunity. No question asked. But, if you have any questions please feel free to ask!"

"What job role are you offering me sir?"

"Postman. I heard you love walking, is that right?"

"Yes… Indeed, I do, indeed."

"I'll take it from here," Cara's boss told the assistants.

Terry's assistants were happy to let the boss lead him into the building. His new boss then took Terry all around the building, explaining what his new job role would involve, the posting routes he'd be taking, and everything else he needed to know. Tears were filling in Terry's eyes and he whimpered.

"What's the matter?" The boss was puzzled.

"No, it's just that… What can I say? Thank you, I…"

"Save that for Cara; she did it for you."

"Can't wait to meet her," Terry sniffed.

The boss smiled.

*****

A few days later, Terry had started settling down in his new job at Royal Mail and was getting used to his new life. He was enjoying every second of it, keeping himself really busy with loads of envelopes and packages until one morning when he looked and noticed a crowd greeting someone. He wondered what all the fuss was about. He didn't realised that it was Cara, who had returned to the job she loved most.

She got a totally unexpected warm welcome from her co-workers at Royal Mail - hugs, kisses on her cheeks, and being given high-fives. She was so happy to be back there again. No one asked about the neck-scarf she was wearing which covered her hidden scars.

Her boss turned up, still looking so nervous.

"Hey," said Cara, giving him a hug, "Thanks for letting me come back."

"Oh, no problem. We all miss you," he replied.

Cara let out a small laugh. Her boss still had crap signing skills; they hadn't changed a bit.

"You're still the same, annoying me, but you're a good boss."

Her boss smiled and said, "Anyway, it's time for you to meet Terry."

Terry noticed his boss approaching him and then he saw Cara's healthy face.

"I believe you two have already met," the boss said, reintroducing them.

"Wow, hello! You're looking good!" Cara said, using mime.

"Thank you. You're looking well..." Terry was almost speechless, "Are you...?" He touched his teeth so that their boss wouldn't understand.

Cara shook her head.

"I owe you a big one," Terry said, changing the subject.

Cara frowned because she didn't get it.

"He... say... he... o-w-e you big." The boss signed using his hopeless signing skills, but Cara got it.

"Oh, don't worry," said Cara. She pointed her index finger at Terry then at herself, squeezing her hand signing 'talk' and pointing her index finger to the side signing 'later' and finally, thumbs up. That was her sign language to tell him: 'You and me talk later, yeah?'.

"It will be great!" Terry nodded eagerly with his thumbs up.

Cara smiled, she felt so heartened, as did Terry. They hugged each other so tightly. Cara was almost in tears but they were happy tears.

"Thank you," he said with the appreciation showing on his face.

"No. *Thank you,*" Cara replied.

Terry smiled, he got what she meant. He wiped away Cara's tears using his thumbs.

"Right. I'm going to work." Cara showed them the envelopes in her hand.

"Go work."

"Yes boss!" Cara looked at Terry and gave him a wink before walking out of the building.

"I'd better get on with it too," Terry told his boss.

"Absolutely. You're a top man, you are," the boss replied as he walked away, trying to look so cool.

Returning to his work, Terry chuckled away to himself; he wondered if Cara was thinking the same about how annoying their boss was.

The boss stopped one of his employees; the 'betting postman' and said, "She hugged me. Now, you *owe* me a fiver!"

The postman winced and forced himself to put a five-pound note in his boss' hand.

CHAPTER THIRTY-SEVEN

Cara arrived home from her first day back at work; she removed her neck-scarf and swapped her uniform for a light vest and shorts before resting in her back garden.

She rubbed on some suncream and laid down, closing her eyes. *Perfect! Hot!* she thought. *Take a nap before ordering a takeaway - double perfect.* She hadn't touched takeaway food since staying at her sister's for almost two months where she ate a homemade dinner every evening. Obviously, she loved her sister's cooking but was in the mood for a Chinese.

Wish I could share it with Sinead, she thought but quickly shook it off, reminding herself of the fact that they *were not* in a relationship.

She sighed and forced her mind to think about getting a tan. *Tan, tan, tan, tan!* She repeated the thought, again and again, *Tan, tan, tan, Sinead...*

Sinead's pale face, beautiful smile on her lips, her brown eyes with shining diamonds hidden behind them. Her short hair.

"Aargh!" Cara grunted. All she wanted was to have a blank mind and to be able to switch off for a bit, but she couldn't. So she just lay there and let her mind battle over blank, Sinead and tan. She knew that she would get a tan by the end of the day anyway.

* * * * *

The curtains in Cara's living room were shut and Cara lay on the sofa watching a lesbian movie on Netflix. The door's light flashed so she paused the film using the remote, put on her neck-scarf, and ran to the front door. Opening it, she looked up in surprise.

"Cara Miles, is this the right address?" Sinead signed, checking her piece of paper.

Cara smiled and crossed her arms before replying, "You know they never say my name every time I order takeaway."

Sinead howled with laughter.

"You work as a deliverer now?" Cara looked Sinead up and down. She was wearing a very casual look - light blue jeans-shorts, a vest and a light jumper for the summer night. *She looks so stunning*, Cara thought.

"No, I just gave the driver a tenner for let me do a role-play."

"A role-play?"

"A terrible role, I know."

Cara laughed.

"How's Terry?" Sinead asked.

"Saw him today. He's... great. Thank you for helping me help him get a better life, really appreciate it."

"No problem."

Cara smiled, feeling heartened. Sinead looked at Cara's neck-scarf and started to take it off. Cara almost stopped her but then changed her mind. She wanted to see what Sinead's reaction would be.

"You still look so beautiful," Sinead signed before removing her own neck-scarf. She also had several scars around her neck.

"You're stunning." Cara smiled again, taking the food order out of Sinead's hand.

"Oi. Where's my tip?" Sinead exclaimed.

"Come in, your tip's inside my living room."

Sinead grinned.

CHAPTER THIRTY-EIGHT
A few weeks later... Dusk.

Sinead and Cara were drinking alcohol inside one of Manchester's Gay Village nightclubs.

They had been a couple since the night Sinead delivered Cara a Chinese takeaway. They kissed.

"I'm going to the toilet," Cara said, desperate for a piss.

"I'm coming with you; I need one too," Sinead agreed.

A few minutes later, they end up shagging in the ladies'.

"Do you feel that?" Cara asked.

"The buzzing?" Sinead replied breathlessly. Cara nodded uncontrollably. "Damn, me too! Want to go home? It's not nice here."

Cara nodded eagerly. They grabbed their jackets and walked out of the ladies'.   Outside the nightclub, Cara saw a man in a vampire costume, wearing face paint and fake fangs. He ran past them. Cara's hands squeezed Sinead's forearm tightly and Sinead yelped.

"What are you wearing that for?!" Sinead shouted at the man whilst trying to stop Cara from hurting her arm even more.

"Stag night and I'm late, man!" replied the fake vampire, still running along.

"That's ok, he's gone. It's not real." Sinead comforted Cara, letting her take her time to let her hands go. Cara had apologies showing on her face.

"I know. Sorry… I can't help it," Cara sighed.

"Don't you worry, babe. Let's go home then." Sinead put her arms around Cara; they chuckled and kissed.

A woman walked along and bumped into Cara's side. They exchanged looks.

"Oh, I'm so sorry!" A beautiful, dark-skinned woman gasped with apologies.

"No, it's fine." Cara spoke with her deaf voiced and smiled.

The woman watched as they walked away, puzzled. She recognised Cara from somewhere. "Hey!"

Sinead groaned, all she wanted to do was go home and have sex with her new girlfriend. She looked behind her, as did Cara.

"I remember you." The woman spoke directly to Cara.

"Me?"

"…Cara?"

"She knows your name," Sinead translated for Cara. Cara looked at the woman, thinking hard but nothing popped into her mind.

"You saved my life a few months ago."

Cara suddenly had a flashback; she saw the thug whom she sucked the blood out of and the woman's terrified eyes. The flashback made Cara's eyes become so wide, "Halle?"

"Yes!"

"Oh my god!" They hugged. Halle laughed, so relieved that Cara had remembered her.

"Looks like you aren't a vampire anymore?" said Halle, looking up and down at Cara's natural skin.

"No, not anymore thank god!" Cara responded.

"Magnificent!"

"It's so good to see you all well!" Cara looked up and down at Halle, "You ok?"

Halle nodded, "Thanks to you."

Cara's eyes filled with tears. "I'm glad. Oh, this is Sinead. This is Halle. Tell her." Cara encouraged Sinead to repeat what she'd signed to introduce them to each other.

"Nice to meet you," Sinead and Halle said at the same time, shaking hands.

"Sorry to bother you both, it's so great to see you," Halle said apologising, "Bye-bye!"

"You're on your own?" Cara puzzled.

"Heh, no, my friends are in that nightclub. I just popped out to go to the cash machine over there," Halle replied, pointing to where the nightclub and ATM were.

"Ok… Please never go alone."

"I won't, I promised you that."

"Alright."

"Bye-bye."

Cara and Sinead watched Halle walking away. Sinead turned to Cara and said, "Nice lady."

"Yeah, I slept with her after I killed a thug." Cara let out a small laugh. Suddenly her eyes widened and she covered her mouth with her hands. "Sorry," she winced.

"Nah - she's fit, I can tell," replied Sinead, looking at Halle's bottom.

"Mmm, she is."

"You know what I'm thinking?"

"Don't know, I'm not a vampire anymore so I've lost my power to read thoughts."

"Halle!" shouted Sinead to get Halle's attention.

"What are you doing?" asked Cara, puzzled.

"Want to join us for a drink at our place?" Sinead suggested to Halle whilst at the same time signing to Cara to 'pick her up'.

Cara realised what Sinead was up to and smiled.

EPILOGUE
Many nights later...

Bob and Jason stood outside, smoking cigarettes and talking about anything other than work.

WHOOSH! A man zoomed out of nowhere which gave both Bob and Jason a scare.

"Fucking hell, what was that?!" yelled Bob, his heartbeat pumping fast.

"What do you want?" Jason asked, staring at the pale-faced stranger.

"Help me," the man said with his deaf voice.

"He's deaf." Bob had realised.

"Help you with what?" asked Jason puzzled.

The man pointed at his arm, just above his elbow. He then pointed to himself, and then at Bob and Jason.

"I'll phone Sinead." Bob dialled her number and put the mobile to his ear. Jason threw down his unfinished cigarette and encouraged the man to join them inside the hospital.

Sinead arrived at the operating theatre two hours later to meet her old friends. "What can I do?" she asked.

"Got us another vampire," said Bob, as he turned his head towards the man. Sinead recognised him.

"Oh, hello," said Sinead and waved at the man.

The man looked back at her in amazement and waved back.

"The 'Very First Deaf Vampire'. How did you escape?" Sinead signed.

That morning - back in the abandoned old mine, Sinead and Cara were getting ready to kill the vampires when suddenly Cara sensed the late arrival of the deaf vampire guy.
Hey!
The deaf vampire stopped in the dark place outside the old mine; he was puzzled. *What? Is it you, Cara?*
Yes, please don't come in - go somewhere dark, but not here. Save yourself. Cara sent her thoughts to him.
He saw the van and realised that Cara was warning him that it wasn't safe for him. *Owe you one,* he thought back to her.
No, you don't. Go! Cara sent her thought back to him. Sinead walked along and ran her hand through Cara's hair, just beside her ear. Cara loved the feeling of Sinead doing that; she looked up at her.
"Ready?" Sinead asked.
Cara nodded.

Sinead frowned, feeling uncertainly, "Cara?"
"Yes, that's her!" replied the deaf vampire guy.
"Ok... How did you drink blood?"
"Rats blood," he said, shrugging as if he had no choice but to do it. "Vegans won't be happy about that, right?"
Sinead let out a small laugh, "Indeed!"

"Can you change me into a human? Please?" he begged her.

"Ok, you have to lie down. It's going to be so painful," explained Sinead.

"Ok... how bad?" The vampire had such a look of anxiety on his face.

Sinead had empathy for him because she remembered what it was like and could picture herself in the same situation.

"Well, if you want to go back to being a human so badly, it will be a worse pain than anything you've felt before."

"I'm up for it; I'm already dead. If I'm dead *dead*, then that's it," he said, shrugging his shoulders.

"I'm here for you," Sinead smiled supportively. Bob and Jason began the same process that Sinead and Cara had gone through before. The deaf guy became so nervous that he gulped and suddenly his muffled voice was screaming.

His eyes and face looked horrified; his face looked like a white full-moon...

CARA & HALLE
(Continue from end of Chapter fifteen)

After Cara found out that she can read Halle's thoughts and send her own thoughts to Halle, she signed, "Right, I better go. You stay home."

"Sorry?" replied Halle. This time she had misunderstood what Cara had said.

I have to go. You stay home where it's safe for you as it's dark out.

"Oh, ok." Halle understood.

Cara turned towards the door and, as she was just about to leave, she 'heard' Halle's thought:

Oh my god her bum! Wish I could fuck her right now.

Cara stopped.

Halle stared at Cara's backside and bit her index finger to calm herself down.

Cara turned her head slowly and saw Halle checking out her ass.

Halle looked up at Cara and realised what she'd just done.

Cara rushed over to meet Halle's lips; they started kissing. She pulled Halle's dressing gown off and then, with Halle's help, took off her own clothes.

"Whoa..." Halle said as she looked up and down at Cara's pale naked skin.

You're so beautiful, Cara thought whilst looking at Halle's dark naked skin.

Halle leant backward on the bed and pulled Cara to her. She noticed that Cara seems so nervous.

It's ok if you don't want to do this, thought Halle, comforting Cara.

Cara held Halle's forearm. *No - just that I'm scared.*

I understand.

Cara kissed Halle's hand. *But I want to... if you want.*

Halle brought her wet, warms lips to Cara's and they kissed. Cara put her leg over Halle to get on top of her.

Can I...? thought Cara, nervously.

Halle smiled, giving her permission for Cara to take control.

Cara licked around Halle's breast. They moaned together while Cara began rubbing her private parts against Halle's. Cara, sucking Halle's nipple hard, was controlling herself to make sure that her fangs didn't come out. She then bit Halle's nipple, carefully.

Fingers please, Halle begged.

Cara stopped where she was and looked up at Halle's eyes.

Are you sure? Cara was very concerned.

Halle touched Cara's cheek and thought, *Are you okay?*

I don't know... Cara's mind went completely blank.

Babe... Halle gulped; she could tell that Cara had become very upset about the flashback of what had happened to Halle earlier. Halle smiled bravely, *Hey, look at me. I'm okay.*

After a pause, Cara nodded. *Alright, but stop me if you don't feel comfortable, ok?*

Halle gulped before nodding. She had complete trust in Cara.

Cara moved her fingers down to Halle's pussy, all the while watching Halle. She gently pushed her fingers inside and Halle gasped quietly. Cara began to move her fingers in a nice rhythm, she noticed that Halle seemed so comfortable but was also enjoying the feeling. Her lips reached to Halle's free nipple and she began sucking it.

"Oh, Cara..." Halle said, moaning with pleasure.

Cara let her breast go and kissed Halle's lips, neck, chest, belly, and continued down until she reached between her legs where she found Halle's wet spot.

Can you change me into a vampire, just like you? Halle wondered, whilst moaning.

I wouldn't recommend it. Believe me... It wasn't nice, not nice at all. Cara responded whilst licking Halle's wet pussy. She licked over her clit whilst continuing to fuck her hard and fast.

Halle could felt her orgasm coming; her wetness went on Cara's face.

It's coming! It's coming! Halle thought loudly, so Cara kept going, her mouth on her pussy and her fingers inside, fucking her until she was screaming. Cara licked her own lips to taste Halle's wetness.

Suddenly Halle pulled Cara towards her, kissing her, and pushed her down on the bed.

My turn, Halle smiled, excitedly.

Cara feared what would happen but felt that she couldn't say no. She'd fucked Halle, so it was only fair that Halle had a turn at fucking her.

Halle put one of her legs over Cara's leg, Cara lifted her free leg so they could rub, pussy-to-pussy.

Cara opened her mouth wide, moaning while staring into Halle's eyes.

After a few minutes, Halle stopped rubbing against Cara's pussy. She moved her face below and started to lick Cara's pussy. Cara tightly grabbed her pillow at the back of her neck, trying to keep herself under control.

Halle was just about to put her fingers inside Cara's vagina when suddenly Cara leant forwards with her fangs showing in anger; it terrified Halle.

Cara realised and shut her eyes.

Sorry Halle... It's just that... Cara couldn't think straight; she was tearful and her breathe was trembly.

That's ok, babe. Tears filled Halle's eyes, they realised that they were both so similar.

Slowly. Please... would you go slowly? Cara thought, looking at Halle.

I'll be gentle, I promise. Cara, realising that Halle was approaching her lips, quickly made her fangs disappear and let Halle kiss her. She kissed her back.

When Halle's fingers went inside Cara, it made her jump a little but she kept herself under control. If she lost control then her fangs would pop out again and cut Halle's lips; she didn't want that to happen. Halle began moving her fingers in and out, in a gentle rhythm.

Cara shut her eyes and wailed inside her mind; her thoughts made Halle cry.

Halle clasped one of Cara's cheeks for comfort.

Want me to stop? Halle thought, asking Cara.

No… don't stop. Can you…. Cara gulped, *can you go…?*

Speed up?

Cara nodded, determined to go ahead with it.

Halle changed the rhythm from gentle to rough.

Cara gasped out so loudly.

THE END

ABOUT THE AUTHOR

EJ Raymond has been proundly deaf since birth. EJ's career is Freelance Artist, actor, BSL promoter, workshop leader and author & scriptwriter. *Dad's Basketball Girl* was their first novel followed by its sequel *Every Father's Nightmare* sequel and *Dusk or Dawn* is their first lesbian novel.
EJ is currently lives with teenage son, Zack.

If you enjoy this book, please leave your feedback on Facebook page, @EJasperAuthor

ABOUT THE ILLUSTRATE

Philippa Tomlin (Phil she/her) is a socially engaged visual artist and theatre maker. With participation at the core of her work, she creates hybrid multimedia public art. Her creative practice has punk roots, and is positive protest, curious and challenging, it brings people together, shares stories and makes positive change. All Phil's artwork is eco conscious, made using reclaimed and recycled materials.

Phil is based in Renfrewshire, Scotland and you can see examples of her process and work via these links: https://linktr.ee/PhilippaTomlin

Printed in Great Britain
by Amazon